KU-223-715

THE POWER AND
THE PASSION

After a failed business venture and a broken engagement, artist Abbie Richards takes advantage of an opportunity to do a year's English teaching in Sicily. There, she becomes involved with the large, extended Puzzi family: its members wealthy and powerfully placed in the community. Abbie enjoys the teaching and the social life at Maria Puzzi's language school, and falls in love with charismatic surgeon Roberto Puzzi, only to find herself dangerously entangled in the Puzzi power struggles . . .

112423101

This item is due for return on or before
the last date below. It may be renewed by
telephone, in person or via the internet at
https://librariesnl.northlan.gov.uk if not
required by another borrower.

North
Lanarkshire
Council

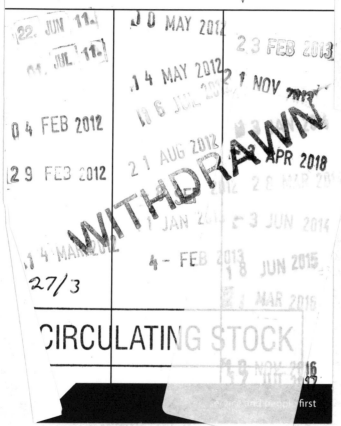

22. JUN 11.

01. JUL 11.

0 4 FEB 2012

2 9 FEB 2012

1 4 MAR 2012

27/3

3 0 MAY 2012

1 4 MAY 2012

0 6 JUL 20

2 1 AUG 2012

WITHDRAWN

1 JAN 20

4 - FEB 2013

2 3 FEB 2013

2 1 NOV 2012

APR 2018

2 6 MAR 20

- 3 JUN 2014

1 8 JUN 2015

MAR 2016

CIRCULATING STOCK

1 9 NOV 2016

serving and people first

SPECIAL MESSAGE TO READERS

This book is published under the auspices of

THE ULVERSCROFT FOUNDATION

(registered charity No. 264873 UK)

Established in 1972 to provide funds for research, diagnosis and treatment of eye diseases. Examples of contributions made are: —

A Children's Assessment Unit at
Moorfield's Hospital, London.

•

Twin operating theatres at the
Western Ophthalmic Hospital, London.

•

A Chair of Ophthalmology at the
Royal Australian College of Ophthalmologists.

•

The Ulverscroft Children's Eye Unit at the
Great Ormond Street Hospital For Sick Children,
London.

You can help further the work of the Foundation by making a donation or leaving a legacy. Every contribution, no matter how small, is received with gratitude. Please write for details to:

THE ULVERSCROFT FOUNDATION,
The Green, Bradgate Road, Anstey,
Leicester LE7 7FU, England.
Telephone: (0116) 236 4325

In Australia write to:
THE ULVERSCROFT FOUNDATION,
c/o The Royal Australian and New Zealand
College of Ophthalmologists,
94-98 Chalmers Street, Surry Hills,
N.S.W. 2010, Australia

JOYCE JOHNSON

THE POWER AND THE PASSION

Complete and Unabridged

North Lanarkshire Council
Motherwell Library
Hamilton Road
Motherwell

	Barcode 112423101
11897101	
Supplier Identity ULV	Invoice Number IS2I7I3
STAT CAT RAFLP	Invoice Date 13/11/11
Price £8.99	Record Number

LINFORD
Leicester

First published in Great Britain in 2009

First Linford Edition
published 2011

Copyright © 2009 by Joyce Johnson
All rights reserved

British Library CIP Data

Johnson, Joyce, *1931 –*
 The power and the passion. - -
 (Linford romance library)
 1. English teachers- -Italy- -Sicily- -Fiction.
 2. Language schools- -Italy- -Sicily- -
 Fiction. 3. Families- -Italy- -Sicily- -Fiction.
 4. Surgeons- -Italy- -Sicily- -Fiction.
 5. Love stories. 6. Large type books.
 I. Title II. Series
 823.9'14–dc22

 ISBN 978–1–44480–567–3

Published by
F. A. Thorpe (Publishing)
Anstey, Leicestershire

Set by Words & Graphics Ltd.
Anstey, Leicestershire
Printed and bound in Great Britain by
T. J. International Ltd., Padstow, Cornwall

This book is printed on acid-free paper

1

Abbie Richards took one last nostalgic look around the bare premises that had been her studio for the last two years — now a dream evaporated into mist. Decisively she slammed the door shut, turned the key and dropped it in her bag to hand in later to the estate agents. 'So that's that;' she turned to her friend, Lisa, 'thanks for working with me and for staying on to clear the premises.'

'Not a problem. I've loved it, though it's sad for you I know.'

Abbie shrugged. 'Inevitable I suppose, but you've been invaluable. You haven't missed London?'

'No, it's been fun working up here. The North East was foreign territory to me. I'm just so sorry things didn't work out for you — with Tim, wretched man! I could murder . . . '

'Ah well,' Abbie quickly interrupted, 'spilt milk, no use crying, better now than later. On to the next . . . um . . . er . . . whatever!'

'No plans?' Lisa put on a woolly hat, fished for her gloves and turned up her coat collar. She shivered. 'And this is summer?'

'Almost. I admit it is a bit bracing.' Without a backward glance at her dream of making a living as a commercial artist, Abbie linked arms with her friend and walked towards the beach road. 'I do wish you'd stay on a bit, I could show you my home patch, have a few days as a tourist.'

Lisa laughed. 'I admit it's attractive, great beaches, wonderful scenery, a lovely change from the big city but . . . oops,' she gasped as they turned to face the biting wind sweeping in from the North Sea. 'Too cold, I'm too much of a softie. Nevertheless I'd love to visit again.'

'Go on, it's beautiful.' Abbie took a deep breath of salty air. 'Um, lovely,' she shouted as a squall of icy rain stung their faces, 'but best leg it to the car park right now.'

The car park was practically deserted, Bolden-on-Sea was a busy coastal resort in high summer but a cold early spring had lowered temperatures to near zero and turned the white-topped sea an uninviting grey.

Lisa's car was nearest, 'In you get, hot coffee in the flask.'

'Phew,' Abbie shook raindrops from her silky hair and unscrewed the Thermos, 'A lifesaver. Thanks.'

'How about a drink at the Northern Lights later tonight? I reckon we both deserve it.'

'We do. I'd love to but I have to get back. Janet, our housekeeper, had to leave suddenly. Her sister in Scotland is poorly.'

'But she's coming back?'

'I certainly hope so, Dad and I would be rudderless without Janet. She's held us together since . . . you know . . . six years ago . . . ?'

'Yes of course. I . . . '

'Don't worry,' Abbie said swiftly, 'we're managing fine. It's just that tonight I'm on hostess/cook duty. Dad's old friend, Desmond Brown, is in town from London on business. He's my godfather, a real sweetie.'

'I remember him. Didn't he and his wife, Catriona, a beautiful, dark-skinned Italian, take us out to dinner in London when we were students — his wife died didn't she?'

'A couple of years ago, really sad. Yes, we had a good time with them. Why don't you join us tonight?'

'I won't thanks, I need to pack my stuff.'

Abbie's face fell. 'Oh so soon? I thought . . . '

'I've things to do in London, but I'll be back. Hey, maybe you could try your luck in the city?'

Abbie shook her head, 'I don't think so, not yet. I'm still reeling.'

'Your dad will help, he's a great guy.'

'He'd love me to join his firm but can

you see me as an accountant? It'd be such a worry for him, he works too hard as it is, poor old love.' She handed Lisa a cup of coffee, 'Careful, it's hot.'

'Thanks, and your dad's not an old love. He's dynamic, handsome, doesn't even look middle-aged.

'He'd be flattered. Oh dear, maybe I should move on. Give Dad a bit of space — it never occurred to me . . . '

'I didn't mean anything . . . '

'Course not, but you're right. Since the accident . . . he and I were a tight small sad unit, Dad threw himself into work and I . . . well I tried to run a business and paint . . . then Tim . . . a disaster . . . '

'As you said, all in the past,' Lisa put in smartly, 'look forward, not back.'

For the last couple of days Abbie had been too busy to worry about her future. On the rare occasions housekeeper Janet Fletcher was away she and her father either knocked up a simple supper together or went to a local restaurant, but tonight was special, a visit from Godfather Desmond was an occasion, especially as they hadn't seen him for over a year.

'We'll take him to Tucker's,' her father had said the previous evening.

'No, I'll cook,' Abbie replied firmly, 'I'm sure Desmond will have had his fill of posh restaurants for business dinners. I'll do something.'

Andrew Richards was doubtful. 'If Janet was here she'd . . . '

'Well, she's not here and I can cook. Now I'm out of a job and I need the practice. I'll do an Italian in memory of Catriona, I remember that Desmond loved her Italian specialities.'

'Do you think that maybe it would be a bit tactless?'

'No I don't. Desmond likes us to remember Catriona, it's hurtful when people pretend the dead person never existed . . . Oh Dad I . . . ' his stricken face had stopped her. 'I'm such a tactless fool, of course we'll never forget Mum and my brothers, how could we ever? But Catriona made Desmond promise not to waste his life grieving.'

'Did she? I never knew that. Kathy and I we . . . we didn't have a chance to say goodbye.'

Abbie put her arms around him. 'I know, Dad. It's still . . . so hard but let's at least be glad Desmond had that chance.'

'Bless you, you're right, Abbie. What on earth would I do without you?'

'Be a lot better off financially for a start.'

Andrew snorted. 'Rubbish, I don't want to hear any more about that. It's over, forgotten.'

'But Tim . . . '

'Stop! That's all in the past, look to the future.'

'Agreed, and maybe Desmond will have one or two new ideas. He has lots of irons in worldwide fires.'

'Somehow, Dad, I don't think business is for me,' she replied ruefully, 'and for now I'll just plan a super supper for Desmond.'

Later in the evening after the studio

closure, Desmond Brown twirled the last piece of spaghetti round his fork. 'This is possibly the best pasta dish I've tasted since Catriona died. Thank you, Abbie dear, and don't you dare tell me it came from the ready made food section of your local supermarket.'

'Course not — that would be no way to repay the wonderful meals you and Catriona used to give me. I do miss those London visits of my childhood, it was so exciting in the big city, you took me to so many things: galleries, theatre . . . '

'It was our pleasure and you'll always be welcome in my house. You know that.'

'Thanks. I'll take you up on that, but first I need to think about earning my living.'

'You don't need . . . ' her father said.

'I do, Dad,' she said sternly. 'So, any advice, Desmond?'

'Well, I'm sorry the studio didn't work out. I heard the bare bones from your father.'

'And I don't want to talk about it any more,' she began to clear the plates, 'dessert's fruit and cheese, and I'll make coffee. Glad you enjoyed supper. 'Hey, I'll cook you a breakfast if you'll stay over.'

'I'd love to but I've an eight o'clock breakfast meeting at the hotel.'

'You have to stay longer next time, we've seen so little of you lately.'

'I know and I'm sorry. The only way I could deal with Cat's death was to fling myself into work, but I'm slowing down now. That's what tomorrow morning's meeting is all about.'

Abbie asked, 'Do you see anything of Catriona's family in Sicily?'

'No, I'm still the untouchable. Catriona always grieved, but we had to accept it. Now though, er, now there is something, um . . . ' his speech became more hesitant ' . . . and I did wonder, hearing Abbie's, um, situation that it might be appropriate . . . ' He floundered to a full stop and threw Andrew an anxious look, 'You see, how would you feel if Abbie . . . ?' He paused again.

'Goodness Desmond, do spit it out. I've never known you so hesitant. Whatever is it?' Puzzled, Abbie looked from one to the other.

Desmond was looking so questioningly at Abbie she began to feel uncomfortable. 'Look, it sounds like something private.'

'No, it's not private, anything but, but maybe you could give us a few minutes alone. I'll talk to Andrew and if he thinks it's a bad idea, well then, that's that. I promise I'll explain later.'

She kissed his cheek. 'Don't gossip too long. I'll be back.'

In the kitchen Abbie spooned coffee into the cafetiere and waited for the kettle to boil. It was good to have Desmond visit, good company for Dad. Like Desmond her father had buried his grief in work; consequently business was flourishing, but at a price.

What an idiot. Since the dreadful day which deprived him of wife and sons

10

he'd mourned his loss and devoted his life to his remaining child — her! She poured hot water on to the coffee and inhaled the fragrance before banging the kettle back on the worktop.

From the sitting room she heard the murmur of conversation, the level rising as she went into the hall. She heard her father plainly say, 'I'm not sure it would be right, Desmond, she's already had a couple of hard knocks. There was that wretched Tim business, then the studio. I need to be around to pick up the pieces.'

'I'm not suggesting the other side of the world,' Desmond interrupted mildly. 'It's not that far. Lots of flights to Europe.'

'Dad, Desmond,' Abbie kicked open the swing door with her foot, 'sorry I've been so long with the coffee.' She set down the tray, straightened up and looked at the two men accusingly, 'And I couldn't help hearing, you've been talking about me behind my back. Tell me, what is it I'd like to help with?'

2

Ah. Coffee, just what we need. Thank you, Abbie,' Andrew took the tray and busied himself pouring coffee and handing out chocolates. 'Brandy perhaps, Desmond? A night cap?'

'Not for me thanks, I need a clear head for tomorrow. Lots of ends to tie up.'

'Ends?'

'Didn't I mention, I'm handing over one of my retail outlets, well, selling out would be a better description? Time I started to retrench, cut back on work, look around, travel.' He picked up his coffee cup, 'New Zealand actually is part of the plan.'

'Of course,' Andrew said, 'I'd forgotten. It just shows how long it is since we caught up with your news. How are Bella and Richard, and the babies?'

'Yes. I thought it was time . . . here,

I've got some pictures . . . '

'Desmond,' Abbie interrupted, 'much as I'd like to see your photos could I ask what you were talking about when I came in?'

'Of course. I'm sorry, Abbie. OK, here goes — now this is just an idea, Abbie, and only because you said you were looking for work and a complete change.'

'I did. I am.'

'Right. Well can I just check, when you were at college in London you did think about teaching at one point? I remember you telling Catriona.'

'Yes, I did but my art tutor was rather dismissive.'

'But you did consider teaching?'

'Yes. I quite liked the idea, even did a crash T.E.F.L. course. A month in the summer holidays. It was fun.'

'Teaching English as a Foreign Language,' Andrew put in helpfully.

'Yes I recognise the qualification,' Desmond said.

'Really?' Andrew was surprised. 'I

wouldn't have thought that was at all your field.'

'No, not mine, but Catriona's sister, Maria, runs a foreign language school in Italy, well Sicily.'

'I never knew that,' Andrew said.

'That's interesting,' Abbie said at the same time. 'It's news to me, no-one ever mentioned it before.'

Desmond sighed. 'I'm not surprised. You see, Abbie, your dad knows a little of this, but unhappily Catriona's family, the Puzzis, disowned her when she married me.'

'No! How shocking. Why? How? What had you done?'

'Nothing, except of course not to be Italian, or rather Sicilian.'

'I don't see . . . '

'Abbie dear, we all belong to the European Union today, have done for some time, but some traditions die hard, Catriona's family was, still is, a very long established Sicilian and extended family of the old guard and wary of outsiders.'

'But Catriona . . . ?'

'Was a bit of a rebel, a modern girl impatient with the confines and traditions of her family. We met in London where she'd been sent on family business.'

'So she was allowed out of the island?' Abbie was wide-eyed.

'Sure, wheedled her way round the old grandfather Puzzi, in spite of her own father, Carlo's, opposition.'

'It sounds very dramatic.'

'It was. Unfortunately for the Puzzis, Catriona met me at a party in London. We fell in love instantly and passionately and she agreed to marry me.'

'And the Puzzis?'

'Forbade it. Sent a male cousin literally to drag her back to Sicily and gave me a very clear warning to keep off or else.'

'Wow!'

'You see they, the family, had arranged 'a good match' with a son of another very old Sicilian family, a good business connection.'

'So how . . . ?'

'Lucky for us this son was of a similar disposition to Catriona. He had his own plans for his future and they didn't include Catriona. So together the pair of them put on a compliant act before both escaping; Catriona to London, the rebel son to America. He'd fallen for an American tourist to the island. Strangely we all kept in touch, he's now a happy family man living in Virginia with a brood of children and grandchildren.'

'Good for you and Catriona. Did they try and find you?'

'Oh yes. We married by special licence and hid out in the Scottish Isles for months. Finally they gave up but only after disowning Catriona and threatening me with a fate worse than death if I ever ventured into Sicily.'

'But when Catriona died?'

'No one came to the funeral. I tried once to see the family in Palermo after her death but it was a frosty experience. I felt . . . well I really felt threatened and I didn't try again.'

'Oh Desmond, how terrible for you and Catriona.'

'It was. It was a shadow on our marriage but we were intensely happy and I still miss her every single day. One of the reasons I'm going to New Zealand is to see our daughter, Bella. Poor Catriona never saw the grandchildren. She died a week after Simon was born.'

'I had no idea of any of this,' Abbie poured herself a glass of wine.

'There was . . . is . . . one redeeming feature. Catriona has a sister, Maria. The brother, Piero Puzzi, totally rejected Catriona, his family pride was outraged, but the sisters loved each other dearly and Maria managed to keep in touch. When Catriona was ill Maria managed to visit us just the once on pretext of some London business connected with the language school.'

'Ah! She has a language school in Sicily?'

'Yes, in Messina. It does quite well apparently.'

'You're saying that a woman is allowed to own — does she own it?'

'Oh yes, she is quite well off. She married Georgio Puzzi, a very distant cousin, but with the same Puzzi name, hence Maria Puzzi still — not a very happy marriage but they have a son, Roberto, a son who apparently inherited his Aunt Catriona's rebellious streak. He left home in his teens, travelled a great deal until home ties pulled him back. I believe he's very clever, a doctor. He wrote to us when Catriona was ill, he intended to visit but something to do with his work prevented him. He wrote again a few weeks ago. He is very worried about his mother, Maria.'

'But what is all this to do with you?' Abbie asked.

'She is Catriona's sister and she was Catriona's lifeline and a possible link which could have led to the family acceptance. That wasn't to be but I feel I have to do something for Catriona's sake.'

'So where do I come into all this? Surely you don't want me to get tangled up in it.'

There was a long pause before Desmond spoke again. 'No, you're right, put like that it was foolish of me ever to contemplate it. I'm sorry, forget it, Abbie.'

'Hey, wait a sec, you can't just dismiss it.'

'Well I thought maybe a spell away from here to forget this awful Tim person and the studio, you having T.E.F.L. qualification, and at least it's something different and Sicily is quite lovely . . . ' He paused before saying tentatively, 'And maybe you could report back on . . . um, Catriona's sister.'

'What? A spy?'

'No of course not. As I said it's a foolish notion, I can't think what I was thinking of — desperation I suppose, it was just . . . Roberto, Maria's son suggested I might go to see his mother but the Puzzi family wouldn't let me get

19

within a thousand miles of her.'

'So why doesn't this Roberto do something about his mother if she's in trouble?'

'I don't know. It's a strange situation, forget it.'

'Hang on, Desmond, easier said than done. Just let me get over the shock. I needn't stay too long, of course that's if I got the job at the school. I've no experience.'

'You have the right qualification, the daughter of one of my colleagues went to Cologne for a term or so. You see they mostly employ young people filling in time. There should be no problem in your getting a job.'

'It's only an idea,' Andrew put in soothingly, 'I don't want you to go obviously, but I thought it only fair to hear Desmond out.'

'Ah, yes, well what an eye-opener. I don't really have to spy though, do I Desmond.'

'Course not. It's just . . . it seemed to fit together when Andrew told me about your problems.'

'OK Desmond, leave it with me. I'll talk it over with Dad.' Abbie's thoughts were whirling; her initial outright rejection of what seemed a very melodramatic idea was being tempered. Maybe it wasn't such a daft notion. Sicily . . . a mission . . . something quite different . . . exciting . . . ?

Desmond looked at his watch. 'Goodness, near midnight I'm sorry I've outstayed my welcome as well as pouring my heart out.'

Abbie stood up and kissed him. She felt she had a mission to go and see for herself. This Puzzi family from the dark ages who had treated two of her favourite people so badly, Desmond and Catriona Brown, nee Puzzi. They had cast a shadow over her godfather's otherwise totally happy marriage.

'I agree, it's been a blight on an otherwise wonderful marriage and I still have its legacy. Bella and the children. I'd go to Sicily willingly myself but I have been warned my life would be in danger if I so much as set foot in the island.'

'So it could be dangerous for Abbie?' Andrew frowned.

'Not at all. I wouldn't dream of asking her to go if that were the case. No, the Sicilians are wonderful people, it's just the family and honour that are paramount considerations, especially to the older long-established families like the Puzzis.'

'Such a story. I can hardly believe it.'

'Let it simmer,' Desmond was shrugging on his coat, 'there's no need for an immediate decision.'

'How do you know I would be suitable for the job? There must be lots of people, especially students, would give their eye teeth for a year in Sicily.'

'Probably, but you would have no difficulty. Roberto Puzzi would be your sponsor and his mother, Maria, would take his word for your suitability.'

'But he doesn't know me.'

'He in turn would take my word for your suitability. They'd be lucky to have you.'

Abbie and Andrew finally saw Desmond to his taxi, waved him off the premises and returned to the house.

'I'll help clear up,' Andrew said.

'No Dad, leave it. Desmond's story is going round and round in my head. Did you know about it?'

'Not in such detail. I knew Catriona was estranged from her family and it caused her much unhappiness. She always dreamt of a reconciliation.'

'It's fascinating. I think I will go — that is if I can get the job at the school.'

Andrew looked alarmed, 'Are you sure? It's a big decision.'

'One thing, Dad, I'd hate to leave you on your own.'

'I'd miss you dreadfully of course, but I've been thinking, it's probably time for both of us to move on. Kathy wouldn't want us to be mourning for ever.'

Abbie put down her wine glass. 'Let's sleep on it then. Maybe this is a good time for both of us to change direction.'

★ ★ ★

Gatwick Airport was crowded with late summer sun seekers. Abbie had made an overnight stop at Lisa's flat and arranged to meet her father and Desmond at the airport.

'What a crush.' She scanned the crowded concourse anxiously.

'End of school holidays, last chance of a family break.' Lisa neatly side-stepped a red-faced toddler trailing a ragged teddy. 'Look, there's your dad and Janet. That tall guy's Desmond Brown isn't he?'

'Yes. Thank goodness they made it though I have already said a lot of goodbyes.'

Lisa waved. 'Mr Richards, over here.'

'Abbie, Lisa, hello. Traffic was terrible and I thought we'd never get here. Desmond insisted on a taxi, good thing as it happened, and how are you, Abbie? All set?'

She nodded. 'Janet, I'm so glad you could make it. You will look after Dad won't you?'

'Away with you, he'll be fine and you just enjoy yourself.'

'I'll try. Dad,' she turned to Andrew, 'you take care, keep up the golf now.'

'I will. I'm enjoying it and Janet's been round with me a time or two. Just for the walk now you understand.'

'I'm his caddy.' Janet laughed. 'But I used to play years ago.'

Desmond drew her to one side. 'Abbie, remember only Roberto knows of your connection to me. His mother, Maria, believes she's simply doing an old friend a favour by giving a job to a friend who's unemployed. If her family learn that I'm involved, well, it wouldn't be good.'

'Yes, yes, you've told me that. Only Roberto Puzzi knows I'm a secret agent!'

'Please don't joke about it. These

25

people can make life unpleasant. You can trust Roberto and he will take care of you.'

A flurry of embraces all round, final waves from the gate and she followed the crowds towards the departure lounge — on her way at last.

The plane was fairly crowded but left on time. As soon as they were airborne she closed her eyes.

A small boy's excited voice jerked her out of her doze. She blinked, aware of clicking cameras all around her. The boy touched her arm, 'Please could we change seats a minute, I'd like to take a picture of Mount Etna, the volcano. He leaned across to look out of the window. 'Look, look, there . . . '

'Should I take it? Probably quicker than changing seats. I'm OK with cameras — honestly.'

'OK here.' He passed over his digital camera. 'Quick though before we pass. Look, it's actually erupting now!' His voice rose to a squeak as Abbie focussed the camera through the window.

'I think that will be a good one. I got Etna dead centre, smoke and all.'

The pilot's voice filled the cabin. 'Ladies and gentlemen, we shall be arriving at Catania Airport in fifteen minutes. Weather — pleasant, 23 Celsius, light breeze. Enjoy your stay in Sicily.'

Abbie leaned back as the plane began its descent, the pilot's announcement had generated a holiday excitement and for a fleeting minute she caught the holiday spirit and almost forgot her mission.

3

Abbie had expected to be met but no-one at the airport had claimed her. It was now nearly two hours since the plane had landed. Either there was some misunderstanding or whoever was to meet her had got lost, or worse, forgotten about her.

Uncomfortably aware she was beginning to attract the attention of some of the male airport staff she decided it was time to make a move. Picking up her bags she walked to the nearby taxi rank. She had the address of the language school, she would go there and hope someone there could direct her to her lodgings.

She chose a cab with a fatherly looking driver, her Italian was good enough for him to understand that she wanted to be taken to Messina.

The driver was about to close the

door when a sleek open-topped sports car screeched to a halt in front of the taxi. A dark haired young man flung open the door, left the car casually parked by a 'no parking' sign and ran towards the terminal. About to enter he suddenly checked his stride and glanced towards the taxi where Abbie was still framed in the doorway. Her driver was standing watching the young man and several baggage handlers materialised from nowhere, anxious to take the man's luggage from his car. He waved them away, came to Abbie's taxi and bent his head to look at her.

'Abbie? Signorina Abbie Richards?'

'Yes.'

'I am so sorry . . . please, come with me. My car . . . ' he spoke rapidly in Italian to the taxi driver and pressed a note in his hand.

The driver nodded, saluted Abbie and returned to his cab with a broad smile on his face.

'Hey, my taxi,' Abbie frowned at the newcomer who took off his dark sunglasses and smiled at her.

'Please, my car . . . '

'But . . . who . . . ?'

'Ah, of course. So sorry, Roberto Puzzi. Many apologies for this unforgivable delay. I telephoned the airport but . . . ' he shrugged his shoulders expressively.

'Roberto Puzzi,' Abbie relaxed, 'from Lingua Puzzi.'

'My mother's school, you have been sent by my friend, Desmond Brown, to teach.' His smile was wide and friendly: dark eyes, tanned skin, white teeth, thick dark hair, an attractive man now holding open the passenger door of his car for Abbie. 'Please, I am to drive you to your accommodation.' Tall, loose-limbed in a white cotton T-shirt and dark trousers he moved like an athlete. His English was near perfect with a slight but charming Italian inflection. 'Is this your first time in Sicily?'

She nodded, 'I've been to Italy before, Florence, Venice.'

'Ah, but Sicily is special. You will see.'

He started the engine, 'I think it will be too late this evening to meet my mother, your employer. I will take you in the morning, the school term starts I think in a day or so. Some staff have already arrived so you may meet them today.'

Abbie glanced at his profile, the warm wind ruffled his dark hair as he turned his head briefly and smiled.

Suddenly there was a roar of a raucous horn as a speeding motorbike swept past them. Simultaneously Roberto flicked a switch and the car hood purred noiselessly over their heads cocooning them in air conditioned luxury. Abbie felt a slight movement in the pit of her stomach as he turned to look at her.

'Sorry, just a precaution. There have been a spate of hold ups and robberies on this road, especially tourists in hire cars. Motor cyclists smash car windows and snatch bags but the police are on to it now and it's been much quieter for a while.'

'Glad to hear it, but isn't Sicily

always quiet and peaceful?'

He laughed, 'Like everywhere in the world there are black spots, bad people, Palermo has a bad reputation. In England too.'

'You've spent time in England?'

He laughed, 'Many years. I trained in London.'

'Trained?'

'I'm a doctor. I did locum work in Newcastle.'

'But you live here now?'

'On and off. I return frequently to England. I'm, how to you call it, a rolling boulder?'

'Stone actually, but I have a rolling stone friend at home. She saw me off at the airport along with Desmond, Catriona's husband.'

'Yes. Of course I know Desmond, he is my uncle by marriage.' For a second he took his eyes off the road to look at Abbie, 'We must talk before you meet my mother, Signora Puzzi. She knows nothing of your connection with Desmond, I hope you can respect that.'

'Of course. My godfather explained the situation to me. I need to . . . er . . . observe your mother . . . not to spy on her of course.'

'Heavens no.' His eyes narrowed and he said quickly, 'My mother is very proud, a very unusual woman, she built up Lingua Puzzi entirely on her own and not without family opposition. She has been . . . IS very successful but lately she has not been herself, something troubles her, but she will not confide in me or any of our family.'

'Is she ill?'

'No, not ill, but what is troubling her will make her ill so as one of her teachers you will be in close contact with her and her staff. I should be so grateful if you would report back to me anything that could explain her worries.'

'Her husband, your father . . . ?'

'No!' his tone was sharp. 'My father will not be troubled, you will never see him at the school. Report only to me. You do understand, Abbie?'

For the first time his tone was cold and she felt a shiver of alarm. What bizarre errand had her godfather sent her on? 'I understand,' she said calmly.

'Good. You see,' his tone was softer now, 'I am her only son but she will never show me her vulnerability. I am away a lot too, but I will stay in Messina for a couple of weeks while you settle in at the school and you will always have a contact number for me.'

Dusk was falling as he drove from the town into a quiet street of tall shuttered houses and pulled up outside one of the tallest, 'here we are. I am very sorry but I'm already late for an important meeting at the hospital, so I haven't the time to take you to your apartment, but there is a janitor on the ground floor who will help you. I will call for you at ten o'clock and take you to the language school where you will meet my mother.'

He carried her bags up to the front step, 'Two keys, one for apartment number three, the other to the main

building. Thank you for understanding.'
Impulsively he leaned towards her, put
his hands on her shoulders and kissed
her on both cheeks, 'Goodnight, Abbie
Richards, I'm glad you are here.' With a
quick wave he took the steps at a run
and was in his car roaring down the
silent street leaving Abbie feeling just a
little bit lost and lonely.

Inside a dark hall was gloomy and
deathly silent. So much for Mediterranean warmth and sunshine she thought
unfairly. 'Hello,' she called and jumped
when a door opened close by flooding
the hall with light and outlining a dark
figure in the doorway. 'Hah,' she gasped
as the figure moved close.

'Signorina Richards?' a croaky voice
rasped.

Her, 'Si, si,' was answered by a gabble
of Italian which she just about deci-
phered, she was to follow him up the
stairs. Apartment three was off a small
landing.

The man, caretaker, she assumed,
opened the door and stood aside for her

to enter. The large lofty rooms had heavy old furniture, tall windows closely shuttered. The old man showed her other rooms, keeping up a flow of Italian. 'Grazzi, grazzi,' Abbie interrupted and, wanting him to leave indicated the front door and he left immediately but still kept up his flow of monologue down the stairs.

There were two bedrooms, one had clothes strewn on the bed, books on a table. She took her bags into the other bedroom which had a high bed and mahogany furniture. In the kitchen there was an enormous bath tub with old-fashioned claw feet cheek by jowl with an equally old-fashioned cooker. A fairly modern fridge yielded rolls, salami and half a bottle of wine.

Hungry and anxious to explore her new surroundings she quickly changed into bright turquoise trousers and a sleeveless black top. She brushed out her shining silky hair to hang loosely round her face and let herself out into the silent street which, as far as she remembered driving in from the airport, led back into the main thoroughfare of Messina.

What a contrast to the flat's location — here the street teemed with life, shops spilled out bright lights and movement and the entire town population appeared to be out for an airing, smartly dressed and in holiday mood. Groups of men argued, hands flying, talking volubly, and youths gathered around outside cafés or ice cream parlours.

She walked on trying to figure out directions back to the lighted streets but she must have taken a wrong turning. She had no idea where she was and it was growing darker by the minute. What a fool! She closed her eyes, spun around, and started to walk in a different direction. It had worked before, why not now?

She thought she saw lights in the distance but then, to her relief, heard the welcome sound of laughter and voices in English.

'OK, Giovanni's, if you must, but we don't get paid until next month.'

'All right, you stay home, get a take away.'

'Heh . . . mi scusi . . . ' The group sweeping round the corner knocked Abbie off her feet on to the pavement.

'Hey, English, she can't be Italian with that hair. So sorry, let me help you up.'

Assisted by a pair of strong masculine hands, Abbie was carefully set on her feet and offered the support of a muscular brown arm. Raising her head she found herself looking into deep blue sympathetic eyes which, set in a tanned face topped with almost white blond hair, regarded her kindly and with keen attention.

'I'm all right really,' she protested, 'it was my fault. I think I'm lost.'

A cool female voice drifted out of the darkness from the back of the small crowd, 'Bit foolish to be wandering about on your own at night. You are rather conspicuous.'

Abbie made out the girl's long gleaming dark hair partially concealing an oval-shaped face.

The young blond man turned towards the voice, 'Well I don't suppose she wanted to get lost.'

'Oh I'm sure she's right,' Abbie broke in, 'but I've only just arrived in Messina and I just wanted to find a café.'

'Can we help you?' a new voice asked. 'Where do you want to go?'

'Viale Martino. Am I anywhere near?'

'We've all just come from near there. Hey, good heavens, how stupid we are, you must be Abbie Richards, the new teacher.'

'Yes, I'm Abbie. What a relief to find you all. Can you point me back in the direction of the apartment. I haven't even unpacked yet.'

'We can,' said the young man who was still holding on to Abbie as if to make sure she didn't disappear, 'but we're on our way out to supper. Why don't you come with us? You haven't eaten, have you?'

'Well, no.'

'So, it must be Giovanni's because if it's Abbie's first meal in Sicily we can't possibly go to Pedro's Pizzaria,' a warm friendly female voice turned out to belong to a girl with tumbling curls who took Abbie's other arm. 'I'm Friedi,' she announced. 'I'll introduce you to the others when we get to Giovanni's. Oh, that's Nick by the way — your other jailer,' she indicated the massive blond man who was still guarding Abbie's arm.

Giovanni's was certainly different. The clientele was a combination of the chic and the casual. There was a lively bustle and Giovanni, the owner, had greeted them effusively as regular customers.

'Now, before we order we must introduce everyone to Abbie.' Nick seated on her left, had taken charge again. 'This is Toni, she's half Italian, hence the dark hair and sultry look.'

Abbie identified the cool voice that had rather censoriously questioned her wisdom in venturing out alone into the Sicilian evening.'

'Hello, Abbie,' the slow dark eyes appraised Abbie coolly before nodding a greeting.

'And this is Susan, the longest serving teacher in the Puzzi Lingua school. This is her third year — something of a record here.'

'Why, is it so bad?' Abbie's question was apprehensive.

'Nick, don't put her off, it's not at all bad. You'll see soon enough,' Susan on Abbie's right butted in, 'anyway speed it up or we'll never eat, and we're flatmates by the way.' Rapidly she introduced the others: 'Bob, Lucy, Friedi, John — all colleagues. Now please, don't talk shop and let's eat.'

Nick's huge hand had summoned a waiter with a pile of menus and comparative silence fell as they became absorbed in choosing their meals.

'The pasta's great here, home made, and if you avoid fish and meat you can get away with a fairly cheap meal,' Bob, a small dark young man in his early twenties spoke earnestly to Abbie.

Nick laughed, 'Bob's got an accountant mentality, too cautious by far. Mind you he's never broke like the rest of us. Anyway, I'm having cannelloni stuffed with spinach and parma ham AND a fettuccine starter. Come on, Abbie, what are you going to have?'

'I'll try the fettuccine please. It always was a favourite of mine.'

Nick closed the wine list decisively and beamed round the table. 'We'll have two bottles of Chianti Classico as well to celebrate the new arrival.'

Slowly Abbie felt herself beginning to relax in such kind and undemanding company. They chattered together in a friendly way, including her without being inquisitive. She gathered that all of them except Susan had been at the school for at least year.

'How did you get from the airport?' Friedi asked.

'Roberto Puzzi met me, hours late.'

'Lucky you,' Toni was immediately

attentive. 'The signora sent a mini bus for us, but then we did all arrive together. It's one of her little economies — she makes sure we all catch the same plane from Gatwick, which saves transport costs. 'I wonder . . . ' A nudge from Bob shut her up.

'Talking of the Puzzis — here they are.'

Abbie looked up to see Roberto ushering a group of people towards a reserved table in the smaller section of the L-shaped room. He was accompanied by four other people, an elderly couple, a younger man and a strikingly beautiful girl. She clung to Roberto's arm who in his turn held the elbow of the elder woman protectively cupped in his hand. The impression was one of power. All heads turned to watch their entrance and Giovanni himself swept towards them, arms outstretched.

'Signor Puzzi, we are so pleased to see you. You stay away too long. You do not like our spaghetti?' The beam of welcome belied the joking accusation as he clapped Roberto on the shoulder in a fatherly way.

'Of course we still love your pasta,' countered Roberto with a smile, 'I've been away but this evening is my cousin's birthday so we're having a little celebration. Prosecco to start please — well chilled.'

'Of course, it will be at your table immediately. But where is Signora Puzzi — you booked for six people?'

'She was to accompany us this evening but unfortunately she wasn't well enough.'

'I'm so sorry,' Giovanni looked mournful as he ushered them to their reserved table. 'Another time perhaps?'

'Too late to disappear,' muttered Nick as Roberto caught sight of them. He looked quite pleased to see them and if he was put out he didn't show it. His courteous greeting included the whole group, his dark eyes lingering for a fraction of a second on Abbie who was suddenly conscious of her bright trousers and sporty top.

The young girl holding Roberto's arm was dressed in a deceptively simple looking green silk dress which subtly emphasised the voluptuous lines of her young figure and which provided a studied contrast to the cream linen skirt and sheer silk matching shirt of the handsome older woman. It was as though they had deliberately chosen their outfits to provide a complementary picture.

'I'm glad to see you have already met your new member of staff, Abbie Richards,' said Roberto as he paused by Nick's table. 'Enjoy your meal,' he nodded as he went to join his family.

'Well there's a coincidence,' commented Bob once Roberto was out of earshot, 'we hardly ever see Roberto with his family. I wonder where the signora is — probably left at home to do the books.'

'I thought he told Giovanni his mother wasn't well,' Abbie said. 'Who's the beautiful young girl?'

'That's his cousin,' said Friedi. She

45

was about to add more but the food arrived borne in by Giovanni himself and two waiters.

'The fettuccine is delicious,' he boasted to Abbie, 'you are new to Sicily so I personally supervise it and then you will return. Yes?'

She began to relax and look forward to working at the school and to meeting Signora Puzzi, Roberto's mother, in the morning. It had been a good decision to come to Sicily.

4

Abbie was delighted to find Susan was her fellow flatmate in the Viale Martino. The two girls said goodbye to the others and walked back together after supper at Giovanni's.

'Signora Puzzi prefers us all to live on the premises,' Susan told Abbie, 'she owns a small block of modern apartments next to the school.'

'Owns a whole block! Must be rich.'

'I think she is. She owns our house too. I like it here though, more old Sicilian. I'm resisting attempts to move me and besides we're nearer the centre of town where we are.'

'Do we have a choice?'

'Well, we're free agents really as to where we live but the signora applies a little pressure sometimes. I think we're OK for the present as all the school flats are full.' Susan yawned. 'I'm glad you're in the apartment though, it's good to have some company and it can be a bit spooky in the house at times. We'll have a chat tomorrow, I'm pretty beat and you must be too.'

'I was, but I feel wide awake now. I haven't even unpacked properly and I'm seeing Signora Puzzi tomorrow morning.'

'Do you know how to get to the school?'

'No, but Roberto Puzzi is taking me.'

'Is he now?' Susan's eyes widened, 'Lucky you. He's a good guy — unlike some of the Puzzis.'

'Who?'

'Tell you about them another time,' she yawned again, 'We don't see a lot of them but ... ' she pulled a face, 'Georgio Puzzi, Roberto's father, the Signora's husband, is a bit scary, a traditional old Sicilian male — woman's place is at the kitchen sink and in the bedroom and all that!'

'But if the Signora runs the Lingua Puzzi?'

'That's at the heart of the problem. Look, I shouldn't be gossiping, I've been here too long and I should know better. You'll probably never even run into the Puzzi male clan, apart from Roberto, and he's away most of the time.'

Abbie wondered why she unaccountably felt a frisson of apprehension, especially after such a pleasant evening.

'Don't look like that,' Susan put an arm round Abbie's shoulders. 'You'll be fine. We Brits tend to stick together, you won't be involved with the Puzzi clan, and the signora is charm itself,' she couldn't help adding, 'bit steely underneath though. She has to be in her position.'

'What?' But Susan was almost out of the door and still yawning.

'See you in the morning, Abbie. Hope you sleep well. Goodnight.'

Abbie did sleep well, too well. It was only when Susan knocked on her door that she woke to morning sun streaming in through the unshuttered windows.

'Coffee?' Susan was at her bedside, there was a fragrant smell of coffee, 'And it's nearly quarter to nine. I thought I'd better wake you if Roberto is coming for you at ten.'

'So late? Thanks, Susan, I had no idea it was so late.'

'I've made you toast and there's cereal. Pop your dressing-gown on.'

'I'll have a quick shower first if that's OK?'

'Sure. I've been up for a while, I've loads of class preparation to do. The signorina likes to swap us around so one year it's pre-university students, the next local businessmen — never a dull moment. She's quite kind, too, starts newcomers off on the easy classes.'

'Such as?'

'English conversation classes are quite fun, English for your holidays, mainly grown ups who want to learn basic stuff and are looking forward to their vacation trip. I've been here so long I've had every variation.'

'You must like it.'

'I do really. I escaped-from a broken love affair a couple of years ago and now I can't tear myself away.'

'I'm sorry. I know how that can hurt.'

'You do? Well mine was a lucky escape.'

'And mine.'

'Well, stories for a rainy day.' She glanced at Abbie's bedside clock. 'Nearly nine, time to get moving.'

Abbie did just that and was outside on the dot of ten.

The red sports car was on time too. 'Hi, Abbie,' Roberto nodded approval at her smart dark cotton skirt and crisp short-sleeved shirt. Her lovely hair was disciplined into a loose knot away from her face. 'Mama will definitely approve, every inch the school marm.' He opened the passenger door for her. 'You enjoyed the meal last night?' he asked as he drove away from the house.

'Yes, very much. My colleagues were very friendly. I feel quite at home already.'

'Good. Giovanni's is always reliable,

and your flatmate, Susan, is an old hand, our longest serving member of staff.'

'People don't stay long then?'

'On the whole, no. Lingua Puzzi is a sort of staging post between graduation and a serious career, a chance to experience life in a foreign country. Is that what it is for you too, Abbie?' He turned to look at her and smiled.

'Er . . . ' He was undeniably attractive, bound to have a girlfriend, maybe even married. He must be mid to late twenties — a doctor . . .

'Abbie?' he prompted.

'Oh! Well I'm sort of between jobs.'

'Right on time,' Roberto said, then he groaned, 'Oh no, not my Uncle Piero.' He punched the horn as a car sped away from the pavement.

'Your uncle?'

'That black car in front of us, now too far away for me to catch.'

Abbie saw Roberto's expression darken. 'Is it a problem?' She asked. 'Did you want to talk to him?'

'Come on, quickly.' He didn't answer, ignored the few students in the entrance hall, all of whom were studying lists or greeting each other exuberantly. He turned around, 'Quickly,' he commanded almost running down a corridor and then, without knocking, straight into the room marked '*Signora Puzzi — Principal, Puzzi Lingua*'. Abbie followed more slowly and by the time she reached the office Roberto had his arm round his mother's shoulders, holding a small spray in his hand.

'Mother, you are upset, have you a pain, the angina? What did Uncle Piero say to you?'

'Nothing, nothing. Please give that back to me. I wasn't going to use it, I am perfectly well. Piero simply came in to say hello.'

'Come on, Mama, when did Uncle Piero drop in for a pleasant chat? He's upset you again. Why is your spray here?'

'No, Roberto . . . ' she snatched back the spray, 'I was simply checking. Now stop it, we have a visitor.'

'But . . . '

'I said stop,' she gave her son a stern frown. 'This must be Abbie Richards, our new employee. Please go now, Roberto and let me get on with my work. I have an extremely busy week ahead with the new school year starting.' Her sharp tone softened as she touched her son's hand. 'Thank you for your concern, my son, but I can look after myself, and I'm sure you have your own work to go to at the hospital.'

Roberto looked agonised. 'I don't like to leave you.'

'Go!' The command was sharp and Roberto's resistance crumbled.

'All right, but I will telephone you tonight and you will tell me if anything or anyone has upset you.'

'Yes, yes dear, I promise. Please, Miss Richards, Abbie, take a seat. Goodbye, Roberto.'

He had no option but to leave, but he wasn't pleased and he left with a frown which included both women.

Maria Puzzi was an elegant and handsome woman in her early sixties. Abbie saw a striking likeness to her son, the same dark eyes, the same beguiling smile as Abbie now found out as Maria smiled and spoke to her in near perfect English. 'Forgive that trifling domestic, er, incident. My son is devoted and caring, no mother could wish for a better, but lately . . . well he worries about me too much. I apologise again, but now to business.'

Her voice was brisk. 'Welcome to Messina, Abbie, the work here is interesting though at times it can be hard.' Her dark eyes held Abbie's, weighing and assessing and as she spoke the lines of pain and stress Abbie had first noticed fell away to reveal a handsome and clearly once beautiful woman. 'We have a mixed student intake, young students from wealthy families, business men and women, young girls wanting to be nannies. It makes for an interesting mix.

'Sophia, my assistant, will give you

your timetable and show you round the school. Students are enrolling today and classes start tomorrow. I hope you'll be happy here and do not hesitate to see me if you have any problems. Oh, and it is a rule here, fraternising with the students — be friendly by all means but remember this is a business and the students are our clients so it's best to keep a reasonable distance.'

She paused and looked thoughtfully at Abbie. 'I'm sure you won't mind my saying this but you are a very attractive young woman, very English — the, er, more forward of your young men will, I'm sure, try to ask you out. It wouldn't be wise, we are quite traditional here.'

'I wouldn't dream of anything other than a strictly student/teacher relationship.'

'Good. I'm glad that's over, it's common sense but needs saying. Maybe in England it's more relaxed?'

'Perhaps a little.' Abbie wasn't going to admit this was her first real teaching post though she guessed Maria Puzzi knew that from her CV.

'I should love to visit England some day.' Suddenly Maria's tone was wistful — uncharacteristically Abbie guessed.

'You've never been?'

Maria's eyes clouded. 'Once only, very briefly on business, and here I am running an English school.'

'But your English is very good,' Abbie said cautiously, guessing Maria Puzzi was not usually given to chit-chat with her new staff.

'I studied hard at school and then, by myself, and I . . . had a sister who lived in England.'

Abbie felt herself go cold, she held her breath, willing Maria not to go on.

'She married an Englishman but I . . . we . . . the family . . . could not visit. Catriona died some years ago.' Now Maria's eyes were pain filled, 'I wished with all my heart I had visited her in England many times. Now it is too late but I am not giving up my school. Never. Never . . . Catriona would not have wished it.'

Abbie sat perfectly still, fighting back the desire to shout out, '*Yes, I knew Catriona, she was like a mother to me and Desmond, her husband, is my godfather and I loved them both.*'

'Well,' Maria made a big effort to regain her authority, 'I look forward to seeing you in the classroom, I make it my business to sit in on all classes — surprise visits of course.' She seemed to have regained her composure as she stood up to shake Abbie's hand. 'Good luck, my dear, I'm pleased to welcome you to the Puzzi Lingua School.'

'Thank you, Signora. I shall do my best,' but all Abbie really wanted to do was pack up her things and fly back to Newcastle as soon as possible. How could she possibly spy on Maria Puzzi and how on earth could she pretend she never knew Catriona when all her young memories were interwoven with spending so much time with Desmond and Catriona? She'd contact Roberto and tell him the whole plan was unworkable.

She rummaged in her bag for her mobile then realised Roberto had not left a contact number. She had no idea which hospital he worked for. Perhaps Susan would know, or Nick — they'd said they would meet up with her at the school. As she stood irresolute she heard her name.

'Abbie, Abbie Richards, wait.' A tall girl with black hair hurried towards her. 'Please wait, the signora told me to show you round and I have your timetable here. I'm Sophia.'

'But I can't . . . '

'Oh please, it won't take long and it'll be much easier for you tomorrow. Truly.'

'I need to contact Roberto Puzzi. It's urgent.'

Sophie looked surprised. 'I've no idea where he is. Signora will know, shall I ask . . . '

'No, no, it's all right. Show me round the school. Thank you.' Slowly her panic began to subside, there was no rush, she could talk to Roberto later, but as Sophia whizzed her around the classrooms, showed her the staff room and introduced her to other members of staff she grew more uneasy. Everybody now regarded her as a permanent fixture. According to Sophia several staff members had abruptly left at the end of last term even after renewing their contracts for another year.

'At least two women from London,' Sophia prattled on, 'and they really loved it here. One even had a Sicilian boyfriend here in Messina and she was so happy last year. Then she suddenly disappeared, paid a financial penalty too. Signora insists that's always in the contract.'

'Oh, Lord,' Abbie remembered there was such a penalty in her own contract. Desmond had said that he would take care of that should she have to leave for any reason.

'And then a couple of part-timers disappeared without trace. Well, they did write — previous engagement or some such. Signora Puzzi is worried though she won't admit it. Student numbers are down too this term — perhaps just as well as we're short staffed.'

5

The first weeks at Lingua Puzzi flew by and Abbie was soon familiar with classrooms and social areas. She suspected Maria Puzzi had selected easy classes for her initiation.

Abbie soon worked out her own strategies, planned her lessons, and began to enjoy life and work in Messina. During her first teaching weeks Maria Puzzi had glided silently into Abbie's classes, taking a seat at the back and making notes.

At the end of each class her nod of approval told Abbie she was on the right lines, but her smile was distant and Abbie sensed Maria regretted her earlier confidences about her wish to visit England. Something out of character Abbie assumed.

Late one Friday afternoon she met flatmate, Susan, packing up her briefcase.

'Hi, Abbie, you joining us tonight?' A small group of teachers usually met up on a Friday evening to celebrate the end of the working week. There were a few classes on Saturday morning but staff members mostly tried to avoid taking them on.

'I'd like to. Thanks. Giovanni's again?'

'No, we'll show you something different, more basic.'

'Bit of a dump she means,' accountant Dave commented, 'but it's cheap and my pay's down this month.'

'Pay's down?' Now Dave had the attention of every one in the staff room.

'Sure, haven't you read your letters from the signora, hours cut across the board — therefore pay's cut.'

'But . . . ?'

'We're guaranteed surely?'

'We're guaranteed a minimum,' Dave's laugh was hollow, 'and that's a pittance. Don't you lot ever read the small print on your contracts? Our salary, or pay, depends on bottoms on seats.' He pulled a face, 'Sorry, but there it is, falling student numbers, haven't you noticed?'

'My class is huge,' half-Italian Sophia pouted, 'would-be au pairs — they're not easy either, giggle all the time. I'm getting sick of it and if the pay starts dropping I'm out. I hate teaching anyway.'

'So why do you do it?' Nick frowned.

'My parents made a deal, work a year or two then they'll pay for a trip round the world.'

'Lucky you,' Susan said, 'but Dave, it's a bit of a worry for those of us who HAVE to work.'

'You've surely noticed the slide in student numbers,' Dave said gloomily, 'Signora Puzzi runs a good school, but there has been an alarming drop in student numbers, this year particularly.'

'There's bound to be ups and downs in numbers,' Nick said, 'but more worrying for Signora Puzzi is the new language school which opened up on the other side of town.'

'There are more language schools

here but this new one is rumoured to be very well financed, modern — even has a spa, a gym and posh restaurant to attract the wealthy kids who want to swan around Europe — London first stop.'

'It's true then, Nick,' Dave asked, 'or just a rumour?'

'It's true, they've been building it during the summer. Check out their website.'

There was a general exodus from the staff room. Nick and Abbie were the last to leave. 'Time for a quick drink before we meet the others?' Nick looked at his watch, 'there's an hour or so before supper.'

'Why not? It'll be great to sit outside in the sun.'

Abbie and Nick had fallen into the habit of meeting sometimes after classes, usually for a coffee and a talk about the day's teaching. But end-of-week Friday called for a celebratory glass of wine.

Abbie turned to face the sun while

Nick ordered two glasses of Prosecco. 'Mmm,' Abbie sipped the cold sparkling wine, eyes closed, 'wonderful. I can't even imagine Bolden-on-Sea right now.'

'Cold up there, I imagine.'

'Well it can be, but the beaches are fabulous — if it had Sicily's climate it'd be tourist-jammed the whole summer.'

'Winters here can be cold you know.'

'So I'll enjoy the warmth now.' She fumbled in her handbag. 'How much?'

'Forget it, it's cheap enough here. You can pay next time, if there is a next time.'

'OK, but we've a whole year ahead. Lots of next times, I hope.'

'I don't know, if you talk to Susan who's been here more years than any of us, Lingua Puzzi's on the down slide. Susan is thinking of starting her own business back home in London.'

'Really? But Puzzi's seems an efficient set-up.'

'Good teaching sure, but a bit behind the times technologically. No website, very little advertising.'

'Mmm, surely that's easy to do, but I had a terrific website back home — didn't do my business much good.'

'You had a business? You're not a teacher then?'

'I did, but I have a T.E.F.L. qualification, did it in my spare time at art college, just in case. Good job I did,' she added ruefully.

'Art college? You're an artist then? Was that your business?'

Abbie nodded, wishing she hadn't brought it up.

'Wonderful. Is that why you came to Sicily, for landscapes?'

Abbie hesitated, 'Not really. Oh well, I might as well tell you, I tried to run a business in Newcastle, arts and crafts, tourist stuff, landscape, portraits, any-thing — bit of pottery . . . '

'So, shall you go back to that after here?'

'It went bust because my business partner-cum-fiancé ran off with the takings and a sizable sum my dad had put into the business.' She took a large gulp of wine which went down the wrong way and nearly choked her and made her gasp for breath.

'Hey,' Nick thumped her on the back, 'deep breaths. Do you want some water?'

'No . . . fine . . . sorry, it just made me think of Tim, ex-fiancé now of course.'

'I've every sympathy,' Nick said sadly.

'Not you too?'

'Not a business let-down, just a last minute decision by my . . . Katie.' His normally sunny expression clouded, his large hand grasped the delicate glass stem so tightly Abbie was sure it would snap.

'Hey, Nick, take it easy. I'm sorry . . . forget I asked.'

His grip relaxed, 'No, it's fine. Just occasionally I'm overwhelmed with a sort of bitter gloomy sadness, but it was a year ago anyway. Quite funny with hindsight, I knew as I saw her coming up the aisle, she stared blankly at me, then she let go of her father's arm, ran towards me then turned to face the congregation and said,' he laughed, 'Sorry folks, can't do it, big mistake, best to admit it now.' She simply ran out of the church and I've never seen her since.'

'Wow . . . that was . . . er . . . '

'High drama to say the least. All for the best probably, hurt pride of course, but Katie's in the States I hear doing a fantastic job in high finance. I'd never have lived up to her lifestyle.'

'It hurts, doesn't it?' Abbie's deep blue eyes were warm with sympathy. Nick instinctively reached for her hand. She closed it over his.

'Hi, you two, two birds with one boulder . . . ah, stone,' the perfect English with only a hint of Italian, 'What a coincidence. May I?' Roberto Puzzi pulled out a chair, 'but first may I get you both a drink?'

'Roberto,' Nick released Abbie's hand, 'how on earth did you find us?'

'I wasn't looking for you. Truly. My

uncle owns this bar, I came to see him and saw you two out here.' He picked up their glasses, 'Another prosecco?' Both shook their heads. Roberto nodded and sat down. 'Lucky finding you here, Nick, I've just visited my mother. She is not too well but a couple of evening teachers have called in sick. Important class meeting for the first time this evening. I told her to cancel but she wouldn't hear or it. Er, is it possible . . . ' he pulled out his mobile phone, 'young businessmen — paying well, could I persuade you?'

Nick and Abbie spoke together, 'I'll do it.'

Roberto smiled, 'Perfect harmony, but I only want one, maybe Nick. No slur on you, Abbie, but these guys are demanding and Nick has more experience — according to my mother. She would be so grateful, Nick.' He glanced at his watch, 'Class is at 6.30, it's only a preliminary meeting, shouldn't take long. My mother believes first impressions are very important.' He smiled ruefully, 'I would do it myself but I wouldn't even know how to start.'

'Sorry, Abbie, we'll talk later. I'll meet you at Catte Negro,' Nick said.

'OK, I'll go back to the flat, pick up Sue and see you later.' She reached for her handbag.

'Ah, Abbie, could I have a word before you go?' Roberto took Nick's seat and waited until Nick was out of sight, 'Abbie, fortunate you were here, too. I'm going to London tomorrow, a medical conference, I'm meeting my uncle Desmond during the conference. I've had an email today — he's worried about you.'

'Why?'

'I'm not sure. You have been in touch with him?'

'I've texted a couple of times, I've been so busy. It's been a bit hectic.'

'I can understand that, and I should have been in touch but . . . '

'You're busy too,' Abbie laughed.

Roberto looked so contrite Abbie laughed, 'Please, I'll phone Desmond this very evening, telling him to stop worrying. I'm a big girl now.'

'But he has known you since you were a little baby? So he can't help it, a part of him still sees that . . . well, the little girl. Whereas I . . . ' he held her gaze, searched her face, 'I see you quite differently. In fact . . . ' Abruptly he stopped. 'I can imagine my uncle could worry,' he finished lamely, 'he has been a lonely man since my aunt Catriona died.'

'Did you see them much in London?'

Roberto nodded, 'They were both very kind, very helpful when I needed help, but you are not interested in our family history, you must go and join your friends. I can reassure my uncle, your godfather, that you are quite well and happy here?'

'I am.'

'And Nick, is he a . . . ?'

'Good friend,' Abbie interrupted quickly. 'Roberto, we teachers have heard rumours of a brand new, language school on the other side of

Messina. Is it true?'

'So I have heard, but that should not worry you at all.' He frowned. 'You have seen my mother?'

'Not often. Sophia has been a sort of mentor. Signora Puzzi comes into my class sometimes to observe. She has made no critical comments.'

'There are none to make, she tells me she is very pleased with you and hopes you'll stay.'

'I'm glad, but Roberto, I still feel quite bad about her not knowing that I'm here under false pretences to observe . . . '

Swiftly he put a finger on her lips, 'Please, Abbie, we've discussed that, it is only a convenience on both sides. Maybe soon you can return to your artist's life.'

'Oh. No, I'm enjoying being here. I've never even thought about painting. The imprint of his finger was still warm on her lips. She caught her breath.

'You should keep it up while you're here. We have fantastic places. I shall take you.'

'Oh no. I'm fine. Really.'

'You don't want me to take you to our finest scenery? Nick perhaps would not be happy?'

'No, no, of course not. Nick is simply a friend that's all. He was telling me his fiancée called off their wedding.'

'Ah!'

'At the altar,' she couldn't help adding.

'So, he will be what do you call it, on the rebound?' He looked at her speculatively, 'You know, Abbie, it's odd, Uncle Desmond, Aunt Catriona, I visited them a lot when I left home. Why did I never meet you?'

'Most of my visits were when I was at art college in the North of England. I didn't have that much free time and before that . . . well, I had to look after Dad.'

'I'm sorry. Yes, Desmond told me about your terrible tragedy. Your mother was an artist, too?'

'She was, far better than I'll ever be.'

'Please, Abbie, when I come back

from London — the autumn here is lovely too, let me show you . . . '

Abbie looked at her watch and stood up, 'Er, it's late, I'll miss Susan if I'm not careful and I don't know where the bistro is.'

Roberto's smile faded, his dark eyes inscrutable, 'Of course, I understand, I am sorry to have kept you. I must go too, I have a flight to catch to London.'

'You haven't kept me. I needed to talk to you, and please give my love to Desmond — and he is NOT to worry.'

Roberto nodded, 'But I see you do not find your situation easy? I must tell my uncle.'

'Please, no. You are misunderstanding me if you think it's OK. I . . . ' she floundered, thrown by the change in Roberto from warm to cool and distant. 'Signora Puzzi is your mother, if you are worried . . . '

'It is my problem, not yours. I now see we, Uncle Desmond and I, were wrong to think of such a thing. I will speak with him. I shall be away for a week.'

'Please, Roberto, you are misunderstanding . . . '

'I must go — my flight. Have a good evening with your friends.' He turned and walked rapidly away.

'What on earth?' Abbie exploded to the empty air trying to fathom what she could have said to upset Roberto. She picked up her bag and tried to look forward to the Friday evening with her colleagues, but Roberto's change of mood had unsettled her, she was glad he'd be away for a week.

Every day Abbie's confidence in the classroom grew and she was surprised how easy she found the actual teaching. She had a natural authority as well as a catching enthusiasm for her subject. She fitted in well with her colleagues too, particularly Nick whose advice and friendship she valued. At the end of her third week she was picking up her papers in the staff room when Sophia came in.

'Ah, Abbie, glad to have caught you. The signora would like a word in her office — ten minutes? She has someone with her right now.'

'Oh dear. Sounds ominous.'

'Oh no, don't worry, she's pleased with you. I think she wants to talk about some private work.'

'Private? No one's mentioned that.'

'No, but it's not uncommon. The signora has lots of contacts in Sicily. Signora Puzzi knows some very wealthy people. Sometimes they ask for one-to-one tuition, intensive stuff.'

There were one or two evening classes starting as Abbie made her way to the signora's office. Maria Puzzi had an apartment within the school and although she owned a villa in the country she spent most of her time in the school apartment. It was well away from the main classrooms and Abbie was still a little unsure of the layout.

One corridor led to a dead end. She retraced her steps and felt certain she was on the right track, especially as she heard voices coming from the room she now recognised as the door to Signora's office. The voices got louder as she approached, she hesitated, it sounded like an argument.

She recognised the signora's voice and a man's deeper, louder voice. The Italian was very rapid, more than one voice, the signora and male voices, sharp, raised in anger above the signora's. Abbie was now at the door, hesitated, raised her hand to knock, but at that moment the voices were louder and threatening. She didn't know what to do, best to go away she thought but as she turned to creep away one man's voice rose to shout, overpowering the signora's.

In an agony of indecision Abbie stood rooted as the door was flung open. Two men, undoubtedly Italian, and one Abbie thought she recognised, the older one, who had driven his car away from the school when she'd arrived with Roberto. There was a younger man with him today, a very worried looking man who tried to calm the older one who roughly shook him off and went storming down the corridor.

The younger man, with dark Italian good looks, shrugged his shoulders at Abbie, looked as though he was about to say something, then ran after the first man.

The door was wide open, again Abbie hesitated, but the signora had seen her and beckoned her inside. She was flushed, breathing heavily, 'Quickly,' she managed to gasp, 'inside, in the drawer.' She put her hand on her heart, pressing it to her side.

Abbie moved quickly.

The signora grabbed the spray and inhaled deeply. It took only seconds before she was able to breathe normally.

'Signora, what can I do?' Abbie was alarmed at the signora's pallor.

'I'm fine. Please, don't fuss.' She swallowed a tablet, closed her eyes briefly, her colour already returning.

'Miss Richards, I apologise, I'm sorry you had to witness the incident.'

Indeed the signora looked almost her usual calm and self-possessed self, still a little pale.

'What I have to say is brief. You have made an excellent start at Lingua Puzzi, the students like you and you appear to work well with your colleagues. I hope you'll stay with us a long time.

'Thank you, Signora. I'm happy here and I'm glad you're pleased.'

The signora looked at her keenly, you plan to stay a while I hope.'

'Well, I don't have any plans for a change just yet.' The twinge of unease at her undercover role persisted.

Signora Puzzi sighed, 'I'm afraid our staff turnover is quite high. I admit staff traditionally regard T.E.F.L. as a sort of station stop before the next move. However, that is a personal choice and I am glad to have you on the staff, Miss Richards.'

'Thank you, I'll try to justify your

confidence in me.' Abbie stood up to leave.

'Just a moment,' the signora's tone was stern, 'I hope you will keep to yourself what you witnessed here. There's nothing to worry about, my own doctor monitors my health so there is absolutely no need to mention this to my son, Roberto. He is not to know either of the visit or my temporary indisposition.'

'Of course, if that's what you wish.'

The signora inclined her head, 'Good,' she glanced at the wall clock. 'Ah, I'm afraid there was another matter I wished to discuss with you, but I have to go out this evening. So maybe in a day or two?'

'Forgive me, Signora, are you well enough? Shouldn't you rest?'

'Heavens no, child. Goodness, I'm made of sterner stuff than that, and don't worry, what I want to talk to you about is a pleasant idea and I think you will like it.'

6

Hard day, Roberto?' In a fashionable London restaurant Desmond Brown topped up his guest's wine glass.

'Thanks. So-so, it's been a packed few days. I'm glad to be having a break from all the medical gossip, though it's been fun.' He raised his glass to his uncle, 'So thanks. This afternoon's speaker was good, very impressive work in Africa, specialises in children's diseases. Running out of funds though — usual story.'

'Maybe I can help and lean on some of my wealthy business colleagues.'

'Really? I didn't mean to . . . '

'No, no, I'd be glad to do something now I'm easing out of the commercial world. Let me have details.'

'I certainly will, and he'll be so grateful. I'm sometimes tempted to do a stint in Africa myself, help spread our medical expertise universally wider.'

'You've travelled a lot since you qualified, lots of locum work. Don't you want to settle down, dare I say it, get married, have a family? What happened to Gina, the one you brought to see us?'

'That was years ago. You trying to marry me off, Uncle?'

'Wouldn't dream of it, but doesn't your native land tug at your heart?'

'Not really. I spent a lot of effort getting away from it remember? I love being in London. I think younger generations in Sicily are changing, eager to leave the nests, signs of rebellion, wanting to escape the older generation for a while.'

'It was a hard struggle for you though.'

'That was mainly Uncle Piero. When my father died I was only ten but Piero took his godfather role very seriously in assuming I was his responsibility. Lots of rows between him and my mother. She encouraged me to take on the outside world and that was the beginning of the antagonism between her and brother, Piero.'

A waiter glided up to their table with a dessert menu.

Roberto shook his head. 'Not for me, thanks.'

'Nor me, that'll leave time to go to my flat, have a nightcap. I've moved to a service apartment, it's only just round the corner.'

'You've surely not sold your lovely house in the country?'

'It's on the market. Far too big for me, and too full of memories of Catriona. I need to travel, maybe new faces and places will help the aching and loneliness.'

'I miss her too.'

'You know Catriona's sadness came from her family alienation, led by her brother, Piero. So it was a wonderful bonus when you visited us so regularly once you'd left Sicily. How are things there?'

Roberto spread his hands. 'OK-ish. I guess I get on well with my cousins and

I don't put up with any attempt to control me by Uncle Piero. It's odd, just because I'm a doctor, a surgeon too, he's just a bit wary of me. I'm the only Puzzi to join a profession, all the rest of them are in building and property development.'

'And the women? Catriona loved her work in the British Museum.'

'My cousin, Isabella, wants to be a doctor. Her father, Piero, would you believe, wants her to marry one of his building chums, stay at home and produce a crèche of male baby Puzzis.'

'Tell her she's very welcome to visit here any time. My sister, Annie, lives in Tufnell Park, she has a big family. They'd love to welcome Isabella.'

'Thanks, I'll keep that in mind. She might well need a bolt hole.'

The two men were out of the restaurant walking along the embankment. They paused to lean over the parapet to watch the Thames slowly glide beneath them.

Desmond sighed, 'If and when I do

move I shall miss this place.'

'No need to make a decision yet surely?'

'Quite right.' Desmond turned away from the river to walk briskly along the pavement. 'Now, Roberto, we've talked about everything but the most important question of the evening. Abbie's father, Andrew, telephoned me yesterday, I told him I was meeting you for dinner. I would have invited him along but he had a prior engagement. Obviously he's been in touch with Abbie: phone calls, e-mails and she says she's fine but he feels she wouldn't want to worry him if she was unhappy. I assume you've met her. Is she truly happy in Messina?'

Roberto thought for a few moments before he answered. 'I haven't seen that much of her. I met her at the airport of course and she has made many friends at the school already, one friend in particular, I think he is very protective of her.'

'Andrew will be glad to hear that, but is she happy?'

'I think she is, she's good at her work, staff and students like her, she is well regarded by my mother but . . . '

'But?'

'Well, I hesitate to say anything because there is nothing concrete, but the school itself has had some problems lately.'

'Oh dear, that is a worry for Maria.'

'It is. Now, Abbie admires my mother a good deal, the way she runs the school, her courage and her authority. My mother, your sister-in-law, is a woman of great strength and spirit. Abbie hates the idea that she is to 'spy' on her employer.'

'Spy! Surely not?'

'The incorrect word, I'm sure. It's possible that Abbie believes she is there on false pretences.'

'Oh dear, I know I should never have suggested it.'

'No, no, you were right to worry, not about Abbie, she is fine, but about my mother. I hadn't realised the pressure my uncle and cousins were putting on her.'

'But why? Isn't it possible to leave Maria to run her school and be happy she is a success?'

'Uncle Desmond, that is not how the Puzzis operate, they don't have a live-and-let-live philosophy, they thrive on power battles and to have these battles you need status and status comes through wealth.'

'Is Maria wealthy?'

'Yes, and in her own right. You probably know she inherited a good deal of money from an American branch of the family. With that money she bought and equipped her language school. She loves the school, the work and the stimulus it gives her. My Uncle Piero wants the school and all its valuable land to develop it as a tourist spa and luxury apartments. He has the ear, naturally, of the local authorities to go ahead. Mother refuses to sell it. Uncle Piero is furious, he sees it as a mission to make her sell by any means, that's the worry, and he has Mafia connections who will do whatever he wants for a price.'

'Mafia? Surely not these days?'

'It's nothing like as powerful as years ago but . . . ' he pulled a face, 'still around, money, corruption, power — not solely confined to the Mafia but they are a force to be reckoned with, dangerous if thwarted.

'My God, Abbie with that lot! She's in danger!' They had reached Desmond's flat and in agitation he fumbled the entry codes. 'I must phone Abbie, Andrew will never forgive me. What's the time difference?'

'About an hour ahead, but no-one's going to touch Abbie. I shouldn't have mentioned the word 'Mafia'. Sorry.'

But Desmond was already hurrying Roberto along towards the lift. Once inside he started a frantic search of pockets and wallet. 'It'll be around eleven o'clock then, not too late.'

'Desmond, there's no point panicking, calm down, Abbie's no fool.'

But with a short run and one bound Desmond was by his front door.

'Desmond, I've got Abbie's number here, let me,' he took the entry key card from his uncle, opened the door and began punching Abbie's number into his mobile. 'It's ringing.' He handed it to his uncle. 'Shall I make coffee? Kitchen?'

'Through there — ah, Abbie, how are you? All right?'

'Desmond, how lovely. Of course I'm all right? Why?'

'I'm worried you might not be painting a true picture to your father.'

'Why shouldn't I? I'm fine, having a lovely time. Sorry about the noise, we're having a party.'

'So I hear. But you're OK? I have Roberto here, we've been out for dinner.'

'How nice. Is he there now?'

'Yes, it's his phone I'm on.'

'Oh, tell him the signora, his mother, is fine, she was at the party earlier, only just left. Hang on, I can send a picture to Roberto's mobile. Just a sec.' Roberto and Desmond heard Abbie organising a group video. 'Quickly, Nick, Sophia.' A few seconds pause then. 'You got it?'

'Yes. Amazing.' Desmond held the phone out to Roberto. 'Looks like they're having a good time.'

Abbie came back into the frame. 'See, all happy and well. It's Mariella's retiring party.'

'Who was the big blond guy with his arm around Abbie?' Desmond asked, peering at the photo image on Roberto's screen.

'That's Nick, one of the teachers at the school.'

'He looks a nice guy.'

'He's OK. You satisfied, Desmond?'

'I guess so. Abbie looks on top form. Hey, what on earth?' Abbie's mobile picture was still on Roberto's phone.

Suddenly the small screen showed uniformed men breaking into the party scene carrying guns and batons. 'Carbinieri, carbinieri . . . ' abruptly the picture wavered then the screen went black.

'What on earth were the police doing at the school?' Desmond looked totally bemused.

'No idea,' Roberto was already trying to re-establish contact. 'No reply, no signal. Try your phone, Uncle.'

Desmond dialled Abbie's number. He shook his head.

'I'll try the school numbers.'

'What about Maria?'

'I'm trying her office. No, only the messaging service.'

'Her mobile?'

'Off too. She'll be on her way home, or at the police station. I'll try a few contacts in Messina, local journalists, and a solicitor who works with the police.'

'I'll get coffee while you're phoning.'

After a few minutes Desmond came back. 'Any luck?'

'No. No news of any police raids on Puzzi Lingua.'

'What shall we do?' Desmond poured coffee with a shaky hand. 'You see, Andrew — terribly tragedy, wife and sons gone in minutes, dreadful boating accident . . . he couldn't take another one.'

'Come on, Desmond, you saw Abbie.'

'Yes but, could you go home, Roberto?'

'What? To Messina? Not until I know a bit more. We can't do anything more, we just have to be patient and wait. I can't leave London until the day after tomorrow, my presentation is the closing piece of the conference. I could . . . ah, good, the phone, probably Abbie telling us it was some bad party joke.'

'Didn't look like a joke to me. They had real guns.' He picked up the phone. 'Abbie? Oh it's you, Andrew, I was going to ring you.'

'Are you all right, Desmond? You sound stressed, bad day?'

'Oh no, fine, and you?'

'I am now. I just had a call from Abbie.'

Desmond shot an agonised look at

Roberto. 'So you know.'

'Know? What? Abbie's fine, I don't think I need worry anymore. She was going to some sort of party at the school, somebody retiring, she seems to have lots of friends so I'm going to stop worrying about her.'

Desmond had put his phone on 'speaker' so Roberto could hear the conversation.

'And there was someone with her called Nick, sounded a nice guy, maybe he can help her forget treacherous Tim. You all right, Desmond?'

'Oh fine, winding down. I've got Roberto Puzzi with me right now.'

'Oh yes, I remember. What does he say about Abbie?'

'Oh, she's happy, doing well at the school.'

'Oh good. I'll be away for a few days, I'm taking Janet up to Scotland to see her sister. We'll get some golf in while we're up there.'

'Sounds great,' Desmond managed to say.

'It will be, oh, and Desmond, thanks so much for suggesting Sicily to Abbie, it's working out just fine, just what she needed.'

Desmond collapsed in to the nearest armchair. 'What a mess! Can't you contact anyone in Sicily, Roberto, find out what's happening?'

Once back in his hotel room Roberto switched on his laptop to check out European news on the internet. At the same time he phoned contacts in Messina. He drew a blank on the internet but well after midnight one of his journalist friends phoned.

'Roberto, Georgio here. I've unearthed the item you're looking for. Late last night, local news, very bizarre. I'm sending it to your laptop now.'

Roberto's screen showed a newscaster who looked quite startled herself as she read out the news item: 'Earlier this evening Messina police raided the premises of Puzzi Lingua owned and run by Maria Puzzi, a member of the powerful Puzzi family. Arrests were

made for drunken behaviour, posses-
sion of drugs, and public nuisance. The
officer involved said it was part of a
crackdown on the growing European
problem of underage drinking . . . ' The
newscaster faded to show a picture of
the Puzzi school in brilliant sunshine
and not a soul in sight.

'And that's it,' Roberto spoke to his
friend on the phone, 'that is just
rubbish.'

'Patience, Roberto, there's a follow
up on the next bulletin, pretty swift
follow up. Here it comes, only an hour
later, a pretty swift reaction from your
mother.'

'My God! Mother!' Roberto turned
up the volume on the speaker. Signora
Puzzi, on screen looking every inch a
very respected business woman stared
sternly into the camera. 'Shortly before
midnight last night I received a phone
call from a member of my staff — a call
from a police cell.'

'Please, not Abbie,' Roberto frowned.

'I repeat, a police cell, where

members of my staff were held for an hour before anyone questioned them. The phone call came to me from Mariella Pablo, a senior member of staff about to retire after many years of wonderful service to Puzzi School. This evening was a private staff party to mark Signora Pablo's retirement — no drugs, nobody was drunk, there was no public disorder.'

'Signora Puzzi,' the news interviewer interrupted, 'how do you account for the police raid then?'

'The chief of police has come up with the feeblest of explanations. I quote, 'a mix-up of destinations, communication breakdown'. No apology for the obvious distress this 'mix-up' has caused to my staff and myself for any damage to the reputation of my school's unblemished record.' The shot faded back to the tranquil picture of Puzzi Lingua in the sunshine.

'Incredible,' Roberto said, 'thanks, Georgio, I owe you. What a fiasco.'

'Difficult to believe but it looks like

your mother's school is a target. Is there some sort of problem?'

'I'm beginning to think so. I need to be home to find out. Anyway, many thanks, you've been a great help.'

Roberto knew that wasn't the end of it. Something was very wrong about the police raid on his mother's school. It was absurd to believe the police would raid the wrong party. There was something sinister and the episode would have taken its toll on Maria Puzzi. Gradually she would be worn down, too ill and too old to withstand the pressures exerted, he was sure, by Uncle Piero and son. No doubt this particular episode would have a cover-up.

No doubt an apology, even compensation, money being no object. But the damage had been done. The clientele of language schools was fickle to a degree and now the name of Puzzi Lingua would be associated with a drunken party.

7

When Puzzi Lingua staff arrived for work the morning after the police raid they found a notice posted in the staff room calling an emergency staff meeting to be held immediately after all classes were over. Maria also gave strict instructions to staff not to discuss the matter of the police raid amongst themselves and certainly not to be drawn into any discussions with students.

The atmosphere in the staff room was subdued but tense and there were one or two grumbles about staying after work.

The people who'd been at the party and at the police station kept a diplomatic silence. Abbie and Nick and one or two others from the party managed to escape for a quick coffee break at lunchtime.

'I wonder how Signora will play it?' Nick said, gloomily spooning sugar into his coffee.

'I hate to tell her but a couple of my students have already left. Brought a note from their fathers, then scarpered.

'That's so unfair,' Susan said. 'The police will have to offer an apology and explain that they'd got the wrong address.'

'Come on,' Dave's brow was black, 'they'll flannel around but won't say a thing. My class was down too, at least three missing.'

'Any excuse.'

'Well, I've had an interview at the new school — it's about to open any day now. At the interview they told me better pay, better facilities all round, great technology, computer centred learning . . . '

'Dave! Surely you're not leaving a sinking ship,' Susan exclaimed.

'Why not? I'm only going to do another year before I go home. Might as well do it in comfort.'

Thus the discussion meandered on until someone noticed it was time for afternoon classes. Abbie felt despondent, sorry for Maria Puzzi. She'd texted Roberto but hadn't had a reply. He must have witnessed the police break-in and be worried sick. She decided to phone him after the staff meeting.

Maria had set up a table in the staff room with wine, cheese and dark Italian bread, a diplomatic gesture which lightened the atmosphere. She waited until everybody had a glass and plate. Abbie thought she looked paler than usual but her voice was clear and strong, her manner confident.

She smiled at her staff and raised her glass. 'Thank you for staying in after a hard day's work. Some of you were at the retirement party, some of you had the unpleasant experience of a few hours in a police cell. I'm sorry for that. I went to the station as soon as Mariella phoned. The police were not too helpful but they did acknowledge they had raided the wrong premises and will issue a public statement to that effect.'

She paused. 'Yes, Nick.'

'Forgive me for interrupting, Signora, but has that been issued today?'

'I haven't seen it, but I have phoned the Chief of Police at intervals during the day, insisting he makes an apology across the media. We shall watch the news bulletins with interest. Susan?'

'I'm afraid we've already lost some students, Signora.'

Maria nodded. 'I'm aware of that. I'm sorry but I've had several parents on the phone today. But we shall survive this totally unwarranted slur on our reputation and I would ask your support and co-operation in now explaining to your classes what happened. Feel free to comment now, or ask questions. Dave?'

'Signora, it does seem unlikely that the police could make such a mistake. Do you think someone is out to ruin your school's reputation?'

There was a water jug on the table, Marie poured some into her empty wine glass and drank a little before answering. Abbie watched her closely; her expression had changed marginally at Dave's question.

'Nonsense, Dave,' she spoke briskly, 'just a matter of police incompetence. Now, please enjoy the wine, I must keep up the pressure on the police. Thank you for your patience.' With an encouraging smile she left the room.

'Well,' Dave helped himself to cheese and topped up a few wine glasses. 'Afraid I'm off as soon as my month's notice is up, I doubt the penalty clause would hold up now. Anyone else?'

'Maybe,' a few murmurs of assent.

Later, a small nucleus of loyalists met up for supper at Abbie and Susan's flat. Nick had promised to throw together a Bolognese, his party piece. Susan switched on the television. 'Let's see if there's anything on the news.' She tuned into the local station. 'Hey, lucky — Puzzi scandal.'

'Puzzi scandal!' Nick exploded. 'Police scandal more like.'

The same Puzzi school picture as the previous evening filled the screen.

A young policeman replaced the Puzzi picture. He read from notes, keeping his head down. The young man spoke rapid Italian heavily accented in the local dialect.

'I can't follow him.' Abbie shook her head.

The apology lasted a couple of minutes only before the policeman, with obvious relief, shuffled his papers together, smiled and faded.

'So . . . ' Abbie asked, 'what did he say?'

'Very sorry, but there's a blanket police initiative to crack down on underage drinking in Messina so hope no damage to Puzzi school, but ends justify the means.'

'Ridiculous, something is going on.' Nick frowned. 'Seems someone wants to sabotage the . . . shush, what's that?' He held up the spoon he was using to stir the Bolognese sauce, 'someone outside.' He quickly crossed the room and flung open the door. 'Hey, what do you want? Why're you listening at the door?'

Susan joined him. 'Oh, that's OK. Nick, it's our concierge, Guiseppe, you know him.'

'I've never found him crouched by a keyhole though. What is it?' But the old man had gone, muttering to himself.

'Was he snooping?' Tom had taken Nick's place at the stove.

'I can't think what he'd gain from it.'

'Oh forget him. Let's eat, I'm starving.' Susan fetched plates and cutlery.

Just as they were starting supper Abbie's mobile trilled. 'Oh sorry, just a second. You carry on, I'll take it in the bedroom. Won't be long. Once away from the others she spoke softly, 'Roberto? Where are you?'

'Not far away. How's Mother? How are you all? Was it dreadful at the police station.'

'Not where I would have chosen to have a retirement party, but there you are, the signora gave us a pep talk this evening but there are defectors. We're having supper, Nick's famous Bolognese.'

'Nick's with you?'

'And the others. It's been quite a day.'

'Hmm, but Maria, my mother, she's all right?'

'Seems to have everything under control.'

'I'll go and see her. I'm at the airport.'

There was a pause, Abbie felt her heart pounding.

'I'll call you in the morning,' Roberto said, polite and distant.

It was well after midnight before Abbie and Susan were left to clear up. 'Two late nights,' Susan said, 'but I feel wide awake. Any wine left?'

After two late nights both Abbie and Susan slept late the next morning. Abbie's mobile woke her. 'Yes, oh, Roberto. Sorry, I've only just . . . '

'Woken up from the sound of it. I'll pick you up in an hour.'

'What for?'

'Saturday. Day off, remember, you don't have a class this morning do you?'

'I hope not, or I've missed it.'

'So, see you shortly.'

Susan brought in a cup of tea. 'Roberto Puzzzi?'

'Mmm. He's coming in an hour.'

'What for?'

'I don't know.' Abbie felt awkward, obviously Roberto wanted first hand information about his mother and the police matter, but she couldn't tell Susan that.

'Exciting? Roberto's a lovely man, cosmopolitan too, but maybe you should be careful.'

'Careful? Why?'

'Well, it doesn't do to get involved with the . . . um . . . This is embarrassing, Abbie, I don't mean to . . .'

'To what?'

'Well, there was an incident here a couple of years ago, great guy called George, brilliant teacher, fell in love with one of the students, she fell for him too but her family were furious

107

when they tried to get engaged. Very wealthy family, had Celia destined for other things. Her family put pressure on Signora Puzzi to sack George which she had to do, but only after a bitter battle. Ironically Celia escaped to the States anyway, married on the rebound, but rumour has it she's very happy.'

'What that's got to do with me.'

'Nothing. Forget it.'

An hour later, Roberto phoned from his car. 'I'm right outside, Abbie. Glorious day, you ready or shall I come up?'

'No, no, don't do that, I'm on my way.' As she reached the hall she noticed Guiseppe's door was ajar, a sixth sense told her he was right behind the door. 'Ciao Guiseppe,' she called out cheerfully.

Roberto, arms folded, was leaning against his open-top car looking up at the building. 'Hi, Abbie,' he greeted her with a friendly embrace and kissed her on both cheeks. 'I'm so glad to see you're OK. Must have been an ordeal for you. Mother's lawyers are working on it.' He opened the passenger door.

'Where . . . ?'

'Mystery trip.'

'But your mother, didn't you come to ask me how she is?'

'I've seen her, she's OK, more depressed than ill though the police raid didn't exactly help her heart condition. So where would you like to go today? Have you done much sightseeing?' he asked as the car moved smoothly through traffic.

'Not really, there hasn't been much time. I've got to know Messina a bit and I've been on a Sunday hike up into the hills.'

'On your own?'

'Oh no, I'd soon be lost on my own; I've got a hopeless sense of direction. Nick was my guide on that occasion, he loves that sort of thing, knows everything about wherever he is. A super tour guide, in fact he's thinking of concentrating on that when he leaves Messina.'

'He is leaving?'

'End of this academic year unless . . . well it depends on what happens to the school.'

'Day off, Abbie, so no more talk of the school.'

'OK, you're the boss.' She settled back to enjoy the ride.

Looking back, Abbie remembered every detail of that day so clearly. She'd seen little of the island apart from Messina and her painter's eyes had been starved of impressions to collect and store for future use. She'd almost forgotten about her other life as an artist in business but the narrow flower-filled streets of that first stop, Taomina, kick-started the artist back to life.

Roberto took her to a main tourist spot, the ancient amphitheatre, the vast space of Greek and Roman origins where opera, ballet and cinema festival were still performed. The weather was perfect, brilliant blue sky hot but not scorching and, as the day wore on just a hint of the colder weather to come.

'Right,' Roberto pushed his hand through his thick dark hair, 'that's enough of the tourist bit. I'm going to take you to somewhere quieter, it's on the road to Etna, so you can take in another tourist Mecca from a distance.'

Now, as Roberto drove up narrow twisting roads the air grew cooler, a faint mist covered the sun. One more twist and turn and she saw a long, low restaurant with wooden deck rails running its length. Its front was turned to the dramatic view of Mount Etna, smoking out puffs of smoke, placid, puffing and peaceful.

Roberto drove into the car park. 'I hope you're hungry. Good hearty Sicilian food here.'

A dark-haired, brown-eyed woman came to meet them, hugging Roberto until he begged for mercy. 'Gina, this is Abbie Richards, from England, a teacher at Maria's school. She needs a good lunch — Sicilian style.'

'Si, si. Pablo,' she screeched, 'Roberto Puzzi's here with a Signorina Abbie.'

A small dark-haired man came running out of the restaurant, embraced Roberto, shook Abbie's hand vigorously, ushered them into the restaurant and seated them at a quiet spot overlooking the rocky vista topped by the quietly smouldering Etna. For a few minutes the three Sicilians spoke almost simultaneously. Abbie heard 'Maria' and 'Piero' several times, stern looks, nods, grimaces, then the trio dissolved, wine and water appeared on the table, a menu was presented then snatched away. An argument between Gina and Pablo then both disappeared into the kitchens at the back.

'Goodness. You know them?' Abbie asked.

'Of course. Gina is my, er, cousin, third cousin, I think, from my mother's side of the family. They're a loving family but,' he sighed, 'you have a family at home in England?'

'Just my father. My mother and two brothers died in an accident six years ago.'

'Abbie, I'm so sorry. I didn't know.'

'Dad and I are very close. It's the first time I've been away from him since the accident.'

'I'm so sorry, Abbie.'

Gina appeared with a laden tray. 'Wine, antipasta, my own baked bread, my speciality lasagne to follow. Eat, eat, you, Roberto do not eat enough, always dashing about. You don't come home enough.'

'I'm fine, Gina. Really.'

'You should settle here, find a nice girl, maybe Signorina Abbie here. Settle down, have babies, be a good Sicilian boy.'

'OK, Gina, thanks. We'll enjoy our lunch.'

Roberto put his head in his hands and groaned. 'So sorry, Abbie, she always does this to me. It was a risk coming here, do forgive me.'

'It doesn't matter, that's what families do, I suppose. Both my parents were only children so I've no close relatives.'

Roberto leaned back in astonishment. 'I can't keep count of mine. Ironically all I ever wanted to do was escape.'

'You seem to have managed that.'

'You have a friend back in England?'

'A boyfriend? No.'

'Hard to believe.'

'I was engaged once but that fell through.'

8

The remainder of that golden day passed like a dream. Roberto and Abbie stayed in the restaurant until the last customer had left. Gina brought a final tray of strong black coffee, tiny delicious cakes and thimblefuls of Amaretto.

It was well into that same evening before Roberto and Abbie arrived back at the apartment. 'Thank you again for a lovely day.' Abbie was loath to break the spell.

'We shall have more days together, Abbie, so many places to show you, material for any artist. I have business in America. I have to go,' his voice was soft and it held a promise as he took Abbie into his arms and kissed her.

'Roberto . . . ' she started to protest but as he held her closer her body began to respond to his kiss. It felt the most natural thing in the world.

'Roberto, I . . . '

He released her but kept hold of her hand. 'Don't say anything, Abbie, just . . . ' he kissed her again, but lightly as in friendship rather than passion. 'Just wait for me until I come back from San Francisco.'

'How long will you be away?'

'It depends. I have a full schedule.'

'Of work?'

'Work and social too. There are things,' he touched her cheek, 'don't dare to leave Messina until I come back.'

He leaned across to open her door and she felt the whole weight of his body on hers. He kissed her lightly on the cheek. 'To the next time, after America. I trust you, and thank you.'

Within seconds his tail light was twinkling in the distance. Abbie stared into the growing darkness watching Roberto's car lights disappear, still shaken by the depth of feeling he had aroused in her.

'Abbie,' a familiar voice made her jump, 'you in a trance?'

'Nick! You made me jump.'

'And you scared the living daylights out of me, standing staring into the night. What've you been doing?'

'Nothing. I . . . Roberto took me for a ride that's all. Come on up, I think Susan's in.'

'OK, just for a short while. I've got masses of work waiting at home.'

As they opened the front door Guiseppe was in the hallway. He muttered a greeting before swiftly disappearing into his own quarters.

'He's a bit odd these days,' Abbie said, 'pops up when you least expect it.'

'Harmless though?'

'Oh yes, completely,' replied Abbie in all innocence.

Next day, Sunday, was a day the Italians promenaded in their best clothes, family parties from grannies to toddlers and babies crammed into pavement cafes, restaurants and ice-cream parlours.

This particular Sunday she felt relaxed and happy, enjoying the company of her

Puzzi Lingua friends. Roberto had phoned her late the previous night thanking her for agreeing to keep a watch on his mother and reminded her he would call her as soon as he was back in Sicily.

'Wake up, Abbie,' Susan nudged her, 'what do you think about the Puzzi party?'

'What? The police raid?'

'No, no, that's history, apart from the fact we've lost a big chunk of students . . . no . . . the Christmas party.'

'Christmas? That's weeks away.'

'Not so long, four weeks. Oh, it's a bit before Christmas but it's the traditional truce when the various branches of Puzzis meet at Piero's country villa, pretend they all love one another, and bring their business associates — i.e. fellow crooks. Only Maria has true colleagues — us. Mind you, it's practically the end of the term by then and some of us are on our way home to Britain. I stay because it's such a great party. Piero Puzzi's villa is really something. You must come, Abbie.'

'I'll see. I'm not sure what my plans are.'

Nick and Susan exchanged looks, Susan was about to speak, but Nick kicked her under the table and shook his head.

'What?' Abbie queried.

'Nothing,' they replied together.

Monday morning brought Abbie back to earth and reality. Sophia came into Abbie's first class of the day. 'Sorry, Abbie, but Signora Puzzi wants to speak to you urgently.'

Minutes later she knocked on the signora's door.

'Ah, Abbie, please come in. I apologise for interrupting your class but this is urgent. I'll be as brief as possible. Please sit down.'

Abbie took the chair opposite Maria Puzzi's desk. For one in a hurry Maria seemed reluctant to begin, then in a rush, 'Abbie, I am very pleased with your work here, so much so I am offering you an unique opportunity to expand your experience.'

'Expand . . . how Signora Puzzi?'

'An opportunity to develop one to one skills — requires a different technique from the classroom.'

'Yes, I know, but . . . '

'I am giving you that opportunity. I think you will enjoy the work — in very pleasant surroundings.'

'Signora Puzzi, are you telling me that you no longer want to employ me at Puzzi Lingua?'

'No, no, what ever gave you that idea? No, you will still be in my employ. An old friend of mine has two young daughters old enough to travel abroad with him. His work takes him to Britain frequently. The girls are clever but their English needs polish. Aldo Zambito has asked me for a teacher and I immediately thought of you.'

'A private class — here?'

'No, of course not. Rosario and Helena have been educated in a private school, they have an excellent grounding, you would give that extra polish, so much so that they could accompany their father on business trips. You would be living in the household as the girls' private tutor.'

'Leave the school here?'

'Not entirely, you will report back here and signor Zambito will also monitor the girls' progress. I will arrange your move to the Zambito villa for tomorrow.'

'Tomorrow? But my classes . . .'

'I will arrange replacements. You will be very happy at Villa Zambito, that I promise you. Also Zambito is one of my oldest friends, as was his wife, Olivia.'

'Was?'

'She died two years ago, Signor Zambito was heartbroken but had his girls to focus on. You will like him, and his charming daughters.'

Did she have a choice? Abbie thought not, and it would be a new experience.

'I hear you are an artist.' The signora broke into her thoughts, 'Rosario is a talented painter, you should do well together. Do you agree?'

'I am your employee, Signora Puzzi,

and I must go where you send me. I will enjoy the experience.'

'Good, good,' the signora glanced at her wall clock, 'and I will be late for my plane to the mainland. Oh, another small matter, Abbie, I hear you spent the day with my son yesterday. I hope Roberto has not been . . . giving you false hopes?'

Abbie's stomach lurched, she desperately tried to control her voice, 'False hopes, Signora??'

'You see Roberto is an attractive man, charming to everyone. Sometimes he may give the wrong impression.'

'I'm sorry, Signora. That is not the case. We are merely acquaintances, your son has been kind enough to show me some potential landscape sketching possibilities that is all.'

'Oh,' Signora exhaled deeply, 'that is good. I should hate there to be any misunderstandings. You see my son, Roberto, is in the States now, his trip is business and pleasure. He is going to meet his fiancée's family, very distant relatives of mine. Petronella is a most suitable match for my son.'

She stood up, smiled at Abbie and shook her hand, 'Thank you, my dear, I'm sure you will enjoy your stay at the Villa Zambito. Carlos will pick you up tomorrow, nine o'clock and he will leave you at the villa for an indefinite period.'

Abbie's head was in a whirl as she automatically returned to her classroom. She couldn't escape the feeling she was being packed off rather like a naughty schoolgirl who had overstepped the mark. A sort of punishment — designs on Roberto Puzzi? That was the implication. Deliberately she shut him out of her mind — engaged!

Tight-lipped, she finished the morning's classes then hurried back to the apartment. Susan, who had the morning free, was surprised to see her and Abbie couldn't help telling her about her meeting with the signora.

'Sorry, Abbie, but I did warn you, very clannish these Mediterranean families, and you did spend the day with him on Saturday.'

'Yes, but that was only to . . . ' of course she couldn't tell her friend the real reason. 'So, how did the signora find out?'

'Got her spies in all places. Maybe Guiseppe. Roberto did drop you off here on Saturday.'

'And Guiseppe was behind the door. Damn!'

'I shall miss you, Abbie, it's been fun sharing with you and I wanted to ask you something . . . ' she hesitated, 'but perhaps not a good time now you're off to pastures new.'

'Come on, Susan, don't be so tantalising. What were you going to ask me about?'

'Ah well, you know I'm leaving Puzzi at the end of the year? I reckon I'm about to start my own school.'

'I know, you've talked about it. So . . . '

'I've done my stint here, I've learned a lot. You're a natural, how about joining forces, starting a language

124

school business?'

'I like that. Thanks, Susan. Let's talk when I come back from the Zambito's.'

Just before dawn the next day a driver called for Abbie. As he put her cases in the boot he smiled, 'Villa Zambito? Ah, Signorina, you've hit the jackpot.'

It was November, the sun was still strong but as the car left Messina and sped towards the hills there was a faint crispness in the air presaging the coming winter. An hour or so later the driver left the main mountain road to travel up towards a villa flanked by cypress trees. A winding drive round the last corner and Abbie gasped.

'Villa Zambito,' her driver announced.

'Wow,' Abbie breathed, taking in the long white building which was flanked by lemon trees, orange trees and, on a slope behind the villa, groves of olive trees. A swimming pool blinked in the sunlight, a young man in white shorts and T-shirt was inspecting the crystal clear water with a long net. As the car drove up to the terrace in front of the villa a man came running down the steps to the car.

He opened the passenger door. 'Ah, Miss Richards, I'm so pleased you are here. Thank you.'

Tall, distinguished, handsome, kindly brown eyes, thick silver hair, tanned, still a young man. Aldo Zambito was a very attractive man.

His smile was warm and friendly. 'I have been looking forward so much to meeting you, Miss Richards.'

'Abbie, please.'

'Here are Rosario and Helena. Meet your tutor, Miss Richards.'

Two dark-haired pretty girls advanced shyly towards Abbie. She spoke to them in Italian. They laughed and smiled. 'Now, English only,' she said, 'during teaching hours.'

They nodded and came shyly to stand either side of her.

'Excellent start,' beamed Signor Zambito.

That excellent start was the beginning of a wonderful time for Abbie.

The villa and its surroundings were outstandingly beautiful, luxury and comfort she had never known before. Her own quarters included a fabulous bathroom and a separate teaching suite had all the latest technology.

The girls loved Abbie and she began to love them too. In the leisure times from study they all three swam together in the clear blue pool, or watched DVDs and movies in the small underground cinema. Aldo Zambito often joined them at the weekend. He was away a lot on business but tried to return most evenings to dine with his girls and Abbie.

The food and wines were delicious and Abbie began to fear she would never be able to adapt to 'normal' life again.

The only jarring note was a succession of texts and e-mails from Roberto. Abbie erased every one without bothering to read them. Nothing was to spoil Paradise, especially Roberto's betrayal, the second in her life. She began to turn to Aldo Zambito for company once the girls were in bed. He was a fund of knowledge about Messina, Sicily, Europe and his library was a cornucopia of entertainment and instruction.

One evening in the library over a late night brandy Aldo talked about his wife. 'Olivia was very beautiful, I miss her so much.'

'I'm sorry, I can't imagine . . . '

'But your mother died you told me, and your brothers. Your father has not remarried?'

'No, but I hope he will. We . . . we became too dependent on each other — it was good to come to Sicily.'

'And good for us too. My girls adore you and they have made incredible progress. I am resisting my friend, Maria Puzzi's order for your return to Messina.'

'She is asking for me?'

'Not exactly. I think my dear friend, Maria, is not happy, her health is worrying. Roberto is still in the States.'

Abbie's stomach flipped.

'Something keeps him there, I believe.' He poured more coffee. 'I hope you will stay as long as Signora Puzzi allows. As you know I am taking the girls to London for Christmas — could you be persuaded to stay until then, maybe even to come with us to London before you return to your home in . . . where did you say? In the north?'

'Bolden-on-Sea.'

'Bolden . . . ? Where is that?'

'Near Newcastle.'

'Ah! Yes, in the er . . . cold and windy area, but beautiful sealine.'

'Coastline. Yes it is, it's lovely, and that's my home. Completely different from here. I shall never live anywhere as glorious as this.'

'I'm sure you will, Abbie. You were made, you won't mind my saying this I hope, made for adventure?' He sighed, 'I envy you your youth and,' he looked directly into her eyes, 'your beauty — both in body and spirit. You have lifted my burden of grief which has been with me ever since Olivia died. I feel we have become friends and if I can ever help you in the future . . . you told me you had a business . . . art . . . '

'Not successful, I'm afraid.'

'Not your fault. I should like to see some of your work one day.'

'Signor Zambito,' Abbie interrupted quickly, 'I have no plans to become a commercial artist, in fact, I have no plans of any kind for the future. I am enjoying my stay here, but it will have to come to an end.'

Aldo Zambito looked at Abbie and again she thought of her father, of course he was an attractive man, just as Aldo represented authority and strength, a rock, a rock who would always be there for her. She dropped her gaze; the brandy, the comfort, the stability of Villa Zambito was beguiling her too much. She stood up, 'Goodnight, Signor Zambito,' she said, 'I have work to prepare for tomorrow. Thank you again.'

9

The Zambito girls could hardly contain their excitement, their father had promised them a cultural trip to Florence to see the art galleries before travelling on to London.

'Please, Abbie, couldn't you come with us, it'll be such fun,' they begged.

'I'd love to, but I must finish the autumn term at Lingua Puzzi.'

'Abbie must honour her contract,' Aldo chided gently, 'it is only right she should do so.'

The girls bid a tearful farewell the day before they left. 'Please, please, come back to us. We'll want to tell you about our trip.'

'I'd love to come again, of course.' She felt a lump in her throat, it had been a blissful few weeks, she'd grown accustomed to the luxury lifestyle. It would be hard to go back to the comparatively cramped Messina apartment. As the chauffeur started the engine Aldo embraced her, kissing on both cheeks, 'My everlasting gratitude for your hard work. Come back soon, there is much that I'd like to discuss with you.' He stepped back as Abbie got into the sleek motor car.

As ever Guiseppe was lurking in the hallway of the apartment block half-heartedly sweeping the stairs, 'Ah, Signorina Richards . . . ' a stream of rapid Italian followed and a sort of grimace that could have indicated he was pleased to welcome her back, but it could equally well mean the opposite.

Abbie smiled and nodded anyway.

There was no question about her welcome from Nick and Susan who were anxious to hear about her luxury lifestyle at the Zambito villa. 'Lucky you,' Susan said wistfully as Abbie gave them a brief outline of life at the villa. 'You were well out of events here. It's been chaos.'

'Chaos? You never mentioned anything when we spoke on the phone.'

'Three members of staff have left to follow Dave to the new rival deluxe lingua and spa, and a fair number of students have defected to the opposition.'

'Oh dear, and the signora?'

'Not good. Several visits from brother, Piero, haven't helped. Apparently rumour has it he really is putting the pressure on her to sell up and retire to her lovely villa in the country.'

'Sell to him of course?'

'Sure. He stands to make a killing; luxury apartments, holiday homes. I'd go like a shot, especially as her health isn't that wonderful.'

'And no problem with planning permission, Piero seems to be able to do just what he wants. I don't know why the signora just doesn't take the money and run.'

'Point of principle to choose her own pathway I guess,' Abbie said.

Susan shrugged, 'I doubt she'll stand

the pressure much longer.'

'So why have so many students left?' Abbie asked.

'Well, the business over the police raid and . . . ' Nick hesitated, 'there are rumours that students are being lured away by rival schools, especially by the new ones, bogus scholarships, bursaries.'

'Wow, that's not legal is it?' Abbie frowned.

'No idea. Anyway there's the pre-Christmas party next week and we're duty bound to go.'

'But if Piero is being so beastly to Signora . . . '

'Don't ask me, I've stopped trying to figure out the rules in these powerful extended families, oh, and the signora wants some of us, including Susan and me to go, and you too, to represent the school at the Puzzi party.'

There was a pause before Abbie could bring herself to ask, 'And how is her son taking this?'

'Ah well, Roberto, it's quite a story

— he's vanished.'

'Vanished?'

'Bit of a mystery, apparently he's lost in the darkest depths of Africa.'

'Africa? I thought he was in the States.'

'Something happened there,' Susan said, 'the signora was in a bit of a temper which soon turned to despair when no one could get in touch with Roberto. Some sort of medical mission, but shrouded in secrecy. Anyway there's a note in your pigeonhole from the signora. I saw Sophia put it in there this morning.'

'For goodness sake,' Nick said impatiently, 'let's forget the Puzzis for a while, the staff, what's left of them, are meeting up to welcome you back, Abbie, at Giovanni's — celebration supper.'

'Lovely,' smiled Abbie, though her heart pounded painfully at the thought of Roberto lost in Africa.

Back at the school next morning Abbie found the note in the pigeonhole summoning her to see Signora Puzzi as soon as she was free. There was also a new timetable, new courses she hadn't covered before which meant more preparation.

For a second her eye pictured Aldo Zambito.

'Abbie Richards, good to see you again,' Signora Puzzi held out her hand, 'you look very well, Villa Zambito obviously suited you and I hear very good reports.'

'Thank you. I enjoyed teaching the girls very much.' Abbie was shocked to see the difference in Signora Puzzi, she looked drawn and tired, her eyes troubled and for a few seconds she stared at Abbie as though at a loss for what to say next.

'You wanted to see me,' Abbie prompted.

'Ah yes, please sit down. Are you happy with your new classes today?'

'Yes, no problems, they are small classes.'

'I'm afraid so, I have had to make

changes in the timetables I'm afraid.' Maria seemed to recover her old self. 'We will soon build up the numbers.' She looked directly at Abbie suddenly sharp-eyed. 'Have you heard from my son at all? I believe you were . . . friendly.'

'Well, Signora, no more than . . . um . . . he showed me the countryside, he knew I was a painter.'

'He took you to my cousin's restaurant.'

'Yes, he was kind enough.'

'Don't worry, Miss Richards, this is not an inquisition, I am merely anxious for my son's safety. He is somewhere in Africa and it's unusual for him not to contact me. I wondered if you . . . '

'No, I've not heard from him, I didn't expect to,' she crossed her fingers behind her back — no point mentioning the texts and messages from America which she had ignored. 'I'm sorry I can't help you, Signora.'

'I had little hope you could but at this stage I am exploring all avenues.'

'Wouldn't his fiancée in America know anything about his whereabouts?'

'That is a family matter, Miss Richards,' she replied sharply.

'I'm sorry, I didn't mean . . . '

'No, no, forgive me, I meant no discourtesy. My mind is distracted, but I must return to the present. You and some other members are to accompany me to my brother's pre-Christmas party, it is customary for a few members of my staff to attend. Piero is very interested in my school.'

This was said so innocently Abbie could hardly believe her ears. 'Why yes, I would like that,' she replied automatically.

'Good. Aldo Zambito and his girls particularly asked me to make sure you were invited.' She rose and extended her hand, 'Thank you again, er, Abbie, and thank you for your loyalty.'

It was after Abbie had left that Maria Puzzi, with trembling hands, reached for her tablets and spray. Her breathing was laboured, her face ashen.

As Christmas drew nearer the remaining staff at the school were very busy with tests, examinations and assessments. Some were leaving the day after term ended and the Puzzi party was a week before Christmas.

There was still no news of Roberto Puzzi and it was now a big media story. It appeared that Roberto and a team of aid workers had travelled to an emergency flood disaster in one of the remotest and most dangerous parts of the country in danger, exacerbated by rivalry between tribes.

As rumours flew the entire Puzzi family became involved. One of their own was missing and however much of a maverick, Roberto was a Puzzi and the family would unite to try their utmost to rescue Roberto from whatever predicament he was in. Piero Puzzi delegated a more junior Puzzi to keep up pressure on Maria to sell her property while he and other senior Puzzis formed a delegation to lobby influential members of the Italian parliament to engage with senior African diplomats to find Roberto and his team.

After a few days of diplomatic pressure, meetings and more meetings, the Italian ministers took the view no more could be done — Roberto Puzzi and his medical team had vanished.

Abbie refused to believe Roberto was lost for good, he was lost to her she knew but some instinct told her he was still alive somewhere. Maria Puzzi's staff were sympathetic but few knew Roberto and their own concern was their own jobs and the future of Puzzi Lingua. Nevertheless the uncertainties generated some tension in the staff room; tempers were short, the usual air of bonhomie missing.

'Hell, I can't wait until the end of term,' Susan flung some exercise books on to her desk in the staff room, 'these results are terrible, I can't motivate these students at all.'

'Never mind,' Nick smiled, 'only a week to the party then we're off home for Christmas. That'll cheer you up.'

'I don't feel like a party,' Friedi said, 'and I can't afford a new dress.'

'Oh, come on, we can all manage something festive,' Susan said as the buzzer went for the next lesson.

Just a week before Piero Puzzi's party Abbie had a call from Aldo Zambito.

'Abbie, how are you?'

'Fine. All went well in London I hope?'

'Excellent.'

'And the girls?'

'Wonderful. You taught them well, Abbie, and they're longing to see you again. Will you be at Signor Piero Puzzi's party? I believe Maria takes along members of her staff who are available.'

'Yes, I'll be there.'

'Splendid. The girls are still in London staying with friends but they will be home for the party.'

'Good. I'm anxious to see them, I've missed them.'

'And they you, they talked of little

else. Rosario did some wonderful paintings of London scenes. They will be in the countryside with friends now until they come home.'

'I'd love to see the paintings.'

'You will but . . . ' there was such a long pause Abbie thought they'd been cut off and was about to switch off her mobile . . . 'Abbie, I should like to take you out to dinner, maybe tomorrow evening?'

'Oh, that's kind but . . . '

'No buts, please. I have asked Signora Puzzi's permission as she considers herself in loco parentis.'

'Signor Zambito,' Abbie said severely. 'I believe I am old enough . . . '

'Just a courtesy,' Aldo interrupted mildly, 'so what does your mind say? I have a proposition to put to you we need to discuss.'

'A proposition?'

'Business combined with pleasure of course. I know a fine restaurant in Messina. I will call for you at eight o'clock tomorrow?'

'Thank you, Signor Zambito, I shall be ready.'

'Aldo, please, and I look forward to seeing you tomorrow evening.'

The restaurant in the smartest part of Messina was busy, Abbie couldn't see an empty table, but Signor Zambito was warmly welcomed by the owner himself who looked at Abbie with great interest.

'So good to see you Signor Zambito, and the lovely young lady. She is not Italian?'

'No. Miss Richards is English, a colleague.'

'Ah yes. As you see we are very busy but I have reserved your private alcove off the main dining too. Please follow me . . . '

'Thank you, Luigi. Very good,' their table was part of the restaurant, but in a discreet corner where the loud chattering in the main restaurant was a mere buzz. Luigi handed menus.

'Please, will you order for me, Signor Zambito — much easier.'

A rapid consultation between the two men, a bottle of wine appeared at the table and Luigi rushed off leaving Abbie and Aldo to themselves.

'Thank you for coming, Abbie,' Aldo poured wine, 'but it can be very noisy in the main dining room and I need to talk seriously to you.'

'Oh dear, sounds ominous.'

'No, no, not at all. First, I want to tell you how well you taught the girls, everyone commented on their command of English, impeccable manners, wonderful hostesses . . . '

'Well I can't take the credit for that, they are so well brought up. May I ask you a question, Signor . . . '

'Aldo, please. You have become part of the family during these weeks. Of course, ask anything you wish.'

Abbie accepted the compliment with delight, 'Forgive me, I realise I've only been in Sicily a short while but you seem very unusual in your . . . well, modern attitude to your girls. I have the impression that women in this part of the world are still usually destined for home and hearth.'

Aldo regarded her with a hint of amusement in his eyes as he commented, 'Now, where have you gained that impression, I wonder?' To her annoyance Abbie found herself blushing, but Aldo continued smoothly as though unaware of her discomfiture, 'It's dangerous to generalise, but I suppose in many families it is true. Not in my case though, and times are certainly changing here nowadays. My wife, Olivia, was a very modern woman, she spent some time in America before we married and I was greatly influenced by her; she was a wonderful, beautiful and energetic woman and we all miss her a great deal.'

He paused, his voice was softer, slower, as he continued, 'Before she died she made me promise to give the girls all the opportunities possible — to prepare for careers as well as family life. I know it's selfish but for a while after Olivia's death only the girls kept me sane. They were my salvation, but now as time goes on and the pain becomes, at least, bearable I must let them go. I've burdened them with my sorrow as well as their own for too long. Your visit has been a catalyst. It's worked, thank God, and I'm overjoyed to see them smiling again.'

His voice broke slightly and Abbie stayed silent, letting the moment of confidences lengthen, not wanting to spoil the intimacy. Aldo's voice was firmer when he spoke again, 'You have magic, Abbie, I haven't talked of this to anyone before but you have brought such light into our house. Maria Puzzi made a wise choice sending you to me.'

'I'm glad too, but what . . . ?'

Aldo held up his hand, 'Let me tell you, you know Rosario has real talent, possibly Helena, too.'

'I believe both of them have great potential.'

'I want to set up a school for artists, maybe Florence or Rome, a cultural centre for struggling artists. I've travelled a lot in Europe with my wife, Olivia, a painter herself. We noticed how hard it was to break into the art world without some sort of patronage. The school would be a philanthropic foundation in memory of Olivia Zambito. Fees would be what students could afford with scholarships and bursaries.'

A waiter interrupted his flow, plates were cleared, replaced and refilled.

Signor Zambito looked at Abbie intently, 'The plan is outline only, does it attract you?'

'Signor Zambito . . . '

'Aldo please. We are friends?'

She nodded, 'I hope so, and it all sounds wonderful but . . . '

Aldo pushed aside his plate and leaned forward, 'Because I should like you to become part of the venture — a business partner.'

'But, I have no money.'

'Abbie,' he said sharply, 'you can't possibly think I'm after money — it's your skills, your teaching expertise, your artistic knowledge, your youth. You would be principal of the Zambito Academy, select and employ the teachers, run the business side with the assistance of a bursar of course.'

'Huh! I've already told you my own business collapsed in debt — I'm a fine recommendation.'

Aldo took her hand, 'Please, stop. You have told me what happened and that's in the past. I'm looking to the future and I think you would be the ideal business partner.' He shook her hand then quickly released it. 'At least think over my proposition, Abbie,' he reached for his case and presented her with a slim folder.

'All my plans are in here. No,' he held up his hand as she started to speak, 'please, let us enjoy the evening — as companions. Read the dossier before you say anything. Now let's enjoy the rest of Luigi's splendid cooking.'

The meal was wonderful, but Abbie

was too stunned by Aldo's offer to concentrate. He was offering a new world, a career in art and teaching, travel. It was breathtaking, she couldn't wait to get back to her apartment and read the dossier.

'I hope this will be the first of many occasions, Abbie. I really missed you when you returned to Messina. I hope that one day . . . '

Luigi arrived with coffee and brandy much to Abbie's relief, yet she didn't withdraw her hand. The warmth of Aldo's hand was still with her when he reluctantly let her go.

To Abbie, Aldo Zambito represented security, warmth and one day a future — his gaze was unmistakable, he would love her as a wife.

She'd thought Tim's love would release her — a very bad error, then Roberto — wrong again. Maybe she was destined to make an unwise choice. Maybe Aldo could be her security, a ready-made family . . . '

'You are miles away, Abbie. I hope I

haven't . . . haven't startled you.'

'Oh no. Really, I'm flattered, and my time at Villa Zambito was one of the best periods of my life since I lost most of my own family.'

Aldo took her hand again, 'Thank you. Think it over, if you like the business proposition I am ready to start anytime, and I'm sure my friend, Maria Puzzi, would release you from your contract. As to the other matter — let your heart speak when it's able. We shall see you at the Puzzi party?'

His manner was now brisk and Abbie began to imagine she had seen love for her in his eyes. 'Yes, of course. The signora insists but she is very strained at the moment. Roberto, her son . . . ' she felt a shock as she said his name.

'Roberto? It's a worrying time but I have no reason, no proof of this, I feel he is safe. Roberto Puzzi is a survivor, but that is no consolation to his mother. Do you know Roberto at all? He's rarely in Sicily except to see his mother.'

'Er . . . I did, because I want to paint, landscape — he took me to see Etna.' She felt herself blushing as Aldo looked at her keenly.

'I should be returning you to your home,' he said quickly, 'I forgot you are a working girl. Maria will not be pleased if I keep you out late.'

'I'm fine, it's not very late and I have all my work planned out for the next few days.'

'See, you would be a model business partner.'

The food and wine had a soporific affect on Abbie as Aldo's sleek motor car purred through Messina's streets. 'Thank you, Aldo, for a lovely meal,' she said as they neared her apartment, 'maybe I should call in at the school and check on the signora before I go to the apartment.'

'I was going to call on her myself on the way back, see if she's in need of company. I can take you to your apartment and return to the school.'

Abbie was suddenly wide awake, a

premonition as a police siren sounded behind them before speeding past. 'It's going to the school,' she cried, 'maybe news of Roberto. Aldo, hurry please.'

He increased his speed but had to slow down as a fire engine screeched past them, all bells clanging.

'It's the school, I know it is. Hurry, please, Aldo.'

'It could be anywhere, Abbie.'

'No, no, look over there, towards the school, that glow. Maria's in there.'

10

As Aldo Zambito increased his speed Abbie gripped her hands tightly together. 'Try not to worry, Maria is probably not in her apartment.'

'But it's in the school building . . . '

As she spoke an ambulance drew up alongside them, two men leapt out and went into the main building where smoke was billowing into the night air. Abbie jumped out of the car and tried to follow them.

Aldo held her back and spoke rapidly to the men and nodded. 'Maria is inside but she's fine. She raised the alarm, there no-one else in the building, they're checking out Maria.'

Within minutes the men returned with Maria Puzzi on a stretcher, protesting hoarsely she was all right, but a paroxysm of coughing left her fighting for breath.

'Maria!' Aldo went over to her.

'Aldo,' she managed, 'And Abbie?' A paramedic put an oxygen mask over her face which she instantly pulled away. 'Abbie's with you?'

'Yes. We had dinner. Don't talk,' Aldo replaced the mask. 'I'll come to the hospital when I've seen Abbie to her apartment.'

'The fire?'

'Under control, some damage, but hopefully not too extensive. Don't worry.'

'Ah,' Maria's eyes closed.

'Aldo, go with the signora,' Abbie said.

'After I've seen you home.' He took her elbow and steered her back to the car.

'Just a second, there's someone over there by the kitchen entrance, looks familiar. He . . . '

'Don't go any nearer,' Aldo held her back.

'It's Guiseppe! What's he doing here?'

'Maybe business with Maria. Don't worry.'

At the front door to Abbie's apartment block Aldo took her key and opened the door. 'I'll telephone you from the hospital if there's any news. A dramatic end to an enjoyable evening. Thank you, Abbie, and I hope to have your decision soon about what we discussed.'

'Of course, and thank you for a wonderful meal.'

'One of many I hope,' he kissed her briefly on both cheeks. 'There is a friend in your apartment?'

'I hope so. Susan, my flatmate.'

'Good. You shouldn't be alone. The fire was a shock.'

'I'm fine, really,' but his concern touched her. Aldo Zambito had strength, authority. An attractive man, she'd enjoyed his company and for a short time that evening she'd forgotten Roberto's duplicity.

Susan wasn't in. A note invited Abbie to join her at the bistro. It was too late to go out again but Abbie was wide awake and restless after her eventful evening. The phone rang — Roberto? But it was Lisa calling from London.

'Lisa, thank goodness . . . '

'Why? What's happened?'

'Well, it's been quite an evening.' She recounted her dinner, the fire . . .

'Wow! Too bad about the fire, but this guy . . . Aldo. How old?'

'His girls are fifteen and sixteen — early forties? No older.'

'Mmm, impressive. What about the other guy, the young one, Roberto?'

'Oh no. All a mistake.'

'You're not seriously thinking about this Aldo guy?'

'Would that be so terrible?'

'So, you're tempted? Well, sounds great.' There was a long pause.

'Lisa, you still there?'

'Yes. Just thinking.'

'What?'

'Somehow not for you. Rebound from Tim?'

'No. No, definitely. No, I'm over him.'

Lisa sighed. 'You're a romantic, Abbie. This Aldo guy, sounds perfect for me, weary old cynic that I am, but there's still room in your life for romantic love.'

'Hmm, we'll see. See you at Christmas, I hope, and you must visit here in the new year.'

'So you're going back?'

'Of course. I've a twelve month contract, and I like it here.'

'I can see that. Oh, and don't forget to report back on that party you told me about. Puzzi mafia?'

'I'm sure that's not true today.'

'Take care anyway.' As Abbie put the phone down a sense of desolation overwhelmed her — at first Tim, then Roberto. Aldo Zambito was balm for the spirit, offering so much, a man who could be trusted. As on cue the phone rang. 'Aldo!'

'Abbie. I promised to let you know, Signora Puzzi is well, a little shocked, the hospital insists on keeping her overnight — a precaution because of her heart condition.'

'That's a relief. Thank you so much.'

'I promised, didn't I? See you at the party.'

Abbie put the phone down. Aldo Zambito, a man of his word, a man you trust with your life!

Next morning Abbie and Susan arrived at the school; groups of students and staff stood around, uncertain whether classes would be running.

'Goodness, Signora Puzzi's here, she must have discharged herself.'

'She doesn't look too bad — she's waving us over.'

As the groups gathered round her Signora Puzzi called for silence. 'Thank you all for arriving so promptly this morning. As you see we had a fire yesterday evening. It was swiftly controlled by the fire services but there is some damage and the building must have a thorough safety check before we will be able to use it.

'As there are only a couple of weeks before Christmas holidays I am closing the school from today. Students should see their tutors this morning when work will be set. Thank you for attending today.'

After talking briefly to individual students Maria joined her staff. 'Thank you all for coming today.'

'Can we do anything to help?' Nick asked.

Maria shook her head. 'The police are investigating, arson is suspected.'

'But you are insured, Signora?'

Maria's face darkened. 'My brother, Piero, dealt with that when I first bought the building — he had contacts . . . ' She paused for breath, hand to heart.

Abbie moved towards her. 'Signora . . . '

'No, please, I am well. Staff who wish to leave may do so without loss of salary. Those wishing to stay for the party at the weekend are welcome to do so and will be welcomed to my brother's villa as usual — and please remember, this accident will not alter the school's future in any way. Thank you again for your support. Now excuse me, I have much to do.' She turned and walked swiftly away.

'A determined woman,' Nick said admiringly, 'and I'm staying for the party, wouldn't miss it for anything. You, Abbie?'

'I think so. My dad's away until Christmas Eve so I may as well stay here, catch up with sight-seeing and shopping.'

In the end about half a dozen opted to stay for the party.

On the day of the party Maria Puzzi ordered a stretch limousine to take herself and the partygoers to her brother's villa.

'Can't imagine why the signora wants to go to her brother's party, they're at daggers drawn,' Susan whispered to Abbie.

'Family tradition maybe, sort of loyalty, but don't let us worry — just enjoy.' She herself felt a flutter of nervousness, Aldo and his girls would be at the party. She looked forward to seeing them but was unsure about her feelings for Aldo Zambito. His feelings were clear but it would be wrong to encourage him unless she could make a commitment.

'Cheer up, Abbie,' Nick said. 'It's a party, not a wake.'

'Sorry. Wow, looks like we've arrived.'

The villa was perched high in the hills above Messina and if Abbie thought Aldo's villa was the height of luxury, Piero Puzzi's was on an even higher plane. Their limousine purred its way through electronically operated iron gates up a long winding driveway brilliantly lit by flaming torches.

As they approached the front entrance the blaze of illumination intensified, lights shone from every window and in a huge gravelled area in front of the house elegant golden lamps and sculptured plinths illuminated sleekly expensive parked limousines.

'Wow,' Abbie breathed in awe.

'Inside's even more amazing,' Susan whispered as they walked up marble steps to the villa.

Inside: soft lighting, music, white-clad waiters with trays of champagne moving discreetly among bejewelled and fashionably gowned women.

There was a reception line to greet the guests, but Maria Puzzi ignored it and went straight to the front gesturing her staff to follow her.

'Watch out for bodyguards,' Nick murmured, 'black suits, silk shirts, no ties, armed and not just with mobile phones and walkie talkies.'

'You've obviously been before,' Abbie put on a bright smile as Maria Puzzi ushered her staff forward.

'Maria, my dear sister . . . ' Abbie caught her breath as a tall elegantly dressed man put his hands on Maria's shoulders and kissed her on both cheeks. Undoubtedly Piero Puzzi.

Abbie could see the family resemblance immediately, he had Roberto's eyes, except Piero's eyes were harder, and his welcome smile failed to reach his eyes.

'Piero, you look well.' Maria was brusque.

'I am, but I hear you have troubles, a fire at the school. I believe.'

'That is . . . ' Maria began as Piero put his finger to his lips.

'Not here, please, Maria, this is the one day of the year we do not quarrel, nor will I refer to our ongoing battle over your school and land. Tonight is for enjoying and you and your staff are my guests of honour.'

Maria, her smile tight, introduced her staff. Piero was charm itself to everyone but when Abbie was presented his expression changed. He gave an imperceptible nod to his hovering bodyguards as he greeted her. 'Signorina Abbie, delighted to meet you, I have heard a lot about you. I believe you have my sister's ear . . . '

'Signora Puzzi . . . no, not at all, she is my employer . . . '

'Mmm . . . and you know my nephew too. We are all praying for his safe return. Please enjoy the evening, we will speak later.' He turned back to his guest line but Abbie saw one of his bodyguards had detached himself from the line and was moving towards the Puzzi school guests.

'Goodness,' she breathed, 'it's all a bit intimidating, isn't it? Signor Piero's a bit scary I think.'

'Powerful presence, eyes and ears everywhere too, knows exactly what goes on in the whole district. It's even rumoured he has spies among the Puzzi school staff. Anyway let's enjoy the evening, it might be our last Puzzi party. Let's dance.' Nick held out his hand to Abbie but a voice behind claimed her attention.'

'Good evening, Abbie, you look extremely lovely.'

'Aldo! And your girls. My, how they've grown.' Abbie was smothered in hugs, kisses and cries of delight.

'Abbie, we've had so much fun, London was amazing and our English was complimented everywhere . . . '

'Have to make do with me,' Susan

said to Nick. 'Looks like Abbie's gone for a while.'

'Could be for good the way that old Italian guy's looking at her,' Nick frowned.

'He's not all that old, a lovely guy, very very rich. I wish I had a chance,' Susan smiled.

Maria Puzzi joined Aldo and his girls as they chatted about their trip; Rosario had kept a scrap book of their travels and Maria began to relax. But she looked tired, worrying about her missing son and the Puzzi Lingua's future. She seemed to accept Abbie as an integral part of the Zambito family and joined them all for supper.

After supper Abbie joined her friends from the school, more dancing, entertainment, music, and all the time she was very much aware of the bodyguard presence. It unnerved her and she was glad Aldo suggested a glass of champagne in the garden.

'Enjoying the evening?' Aldo asked.

'Of course, who wouldn't?'

'And have you thought any more of my proposition?'

'I have, and I've spoken to my father about it. He approves in outline and he'd like to meet you.'

'I look forward to that.'

'In the new year, he'll travel back with me.'

'Good. And my other . . . proposition . . . the future . . . long term?'

Abbie took a deep breath — Aldo Zambito, a powerful, honourable man, kind, wise, a wonderful family. 'Aldo, I can't tell you how honoured I am, but it wouldn't be fair. I like you so much, admire you enormously, but . . . '

'You don't love me. I understand of course, we are spring and autumn, I know that and I understand completely, but there are many kinds of love. There's no hurry, take your time, but may I hope?'

'Ye-es, I think . . . maybe . . . '

'Then I am happy with that. I am a patient man, comes with old age, Abbie . . . '

'But you're not . . . '

A discreet cough interrupted her, a soft voice, 'Signorina Richards.'

She turned, one of the black bodyguard brigade behind her bent to speak, 'Signorina, Signora Puzzi wishes to see you urgently.'

'Is she all right?'

Aldo rose. 'I'll come too.'

'No, no, the signora expressly asked that the lady comes alone. If you'll follow me?'

'But . . . '

'Please, Aldo, I'll come back as soon as I've seen her. She may want to leave, it's getting quite late.'

'I'll get the girls, we'll be in the main hall.'

'Signorina . . . ' the man beckoned her. 'Follow, please.' He moved away from the house towards a dimly lit part of the vast grounds. In her high heels Abbie stumbled, the man gripped her arm tightly. 'Come,' he said.

'Where are we going?' They were well away from the lighted house and garden, no-one in sight. She pulled away, 'Where are you taking me?'

His grip tightened.

'Let me go — now.'

'A moment, signorina.'

By some trees a car, blacked out, engine running, door open. As she struggled the man pushed her into the back, slammed the door and knocked on the driver's window. She screamed, banged on the partition between herself and the driver. 'Let me out,' she yelled, 'who . . . ?'

'Please, Signorina, you are in no danger,' a soft voice carried through a speaker. 'A very short ride, have no fear.' The voice faded, replaced by music.

'For goodness' sake,' Abbie banged even harder on the partition. 'I'm not scared, just furious.' The music continued and she was about to launch another assault on the partition when the car suddenly stopped.

'Journey's end,' the voice said as two men came out of a building. One opened the door. 'Signorina Richards, welcome to Puzzi Lodge. Signor Puzzi is waiting for you.'

'What on earth?'

'Please, patience.' Her arm was firmly held as she was led up into a house, the door shut behind her. 'Please, one more moment,' lights were switched to show a large panelled hall with trophies on the walls. A door at the far end opened, Piero Puzzi came towards her.

'Welcome, Signorina, apologies for the rather unorthodox kidnap, but I wanted to talk to you.'

'Surely there was no need for this charade.'

'Ah well, perhaps a touch melodramatic, but I will explain. Through here please.'

A short corridor to another room, a tremendous buzz of conversation abruptly ceased as Piero Puzzi entered with Abbie. A dining room, a large round table closely packed with people, mostly men, two or three women, ages ranging from middle age to twenties, all looking expectantly at her, all in full party dress.

'My family,' Piero swept an arm round the table, firing off names rapidly, acknowledged by a curt nod from each. 'Please, sit by me.' He patted the seat next to him.

'Is this some sort of joke — a party game?'

'Not a game . . . a consultation exercise. These people are my business associates, all family, all work for family businesses. Many businesses. We control a large part of the town, have done for centuries. The Puzzi word is law.'

'Not with me . . . ' Abbie started.

Piero ignored her. 'Only one thing is beyond our reach . . . '

'I know, your sister's school and its land.'

He nodded. 'Precisely. I have tried for years to buy, offered good prices, up-and-up. She refuses — always.' Now Piero was flushed and one or two listeners shifted in their seats. 'All the people here — all Puzzis have a stake in this, there is a fortune to be made, luxury apartments, a spa . . . '

'But, but . . . ' spluttered Abbie, 'what's it got to do with me?'

'I need your help, you are close to Maria, she trusts you. I know you visit her office, you help her when she is sick, she was in your party tonight, you had supper together.'

'Rubbish, rubbish, Signor. I don't want to be rude as I am a guest at your party, or rather a kidnapped one now, but I have no influence whatever on Signora Puzzi's decisions. You have been misinformed and even if I had any influence with your sister I would strongly advise her to be her own woman and do whatever she wants to do. She loves the school, she has a place in the world and you,' she swept her eyes round the table, 'you all should respect that right.'

'You know nothing of our culture,' Piero spat out, 'family solidarity is our law, my word as family head is law.' One or two younger heads looked up with a frown, a few more shuffled and looked uneasy.

Abbie saw her advantage, 'Signor, forgive me, but this is the 21st century, I don't presume to question your authority, but surely . . . ' she blinked as Piero banged his fist on the table.

'Don't dare fight with me, Signorina, you are a long way from the house and I could keep you here until . . . ' but Piero's anger was beginning to lose steam as there were one or two murmurs of dissent.

'Don't be ridiculous, Signor Puzzi, my friends and the signora will be looking for me. I am leaving now, either on my own, or will I beg the courtesy of one of your family to take me back to your villa.'

For five seconds there was silence then two young men and one woman got up. 'I will take you . . . ' all three spoke.

Piero glared and stamped his foot but before he could speak, a black suited bodyguard rushed into the room waving his mobile phone. 'Signor Puzzi, news, news. Your nephew, Roberto Puzzi, is found, is here, is at the villa. Now, all come . . .'

Abbie would never forget the next scene in the drama, stunned silence, then cheers, hugging, waving and shouting. Several hugged her, one young man whispered in her ear. 'Thank you, thank you, you are the breakthrough, he will never be as powerful again.'

Piero firmly held up his hand. 'Meeting adjourned, but,' he glared, 'not abandoned. Now we can welcome back one of our own.' He stormed out but only a few of the older men followed him immediately.

Abbie had half a dozen offers of lifts back to the villa which was in fact only a five minute drive away. She drove with the younger members who all chattered excitedly about the evening. Their Italian was far to rapid for her to follow, she only gathered they were pleased with her stand against Piero and several of them sympathised with Maria.

As they drew near the villa all Abbie could think was that shortly she would inevitably be face-to-face with Roberto Puzzi, and her heart was in turmoil.

The scene outside the Puzzi villa was a sharp contrast to that of their arrival. Now cars parked anywhere in the grounds as news spread in the town of Roberto's arrival at the villa. Firecrackers cracked open the night sky into rainbows of sparkly colours.

Abbie could hardly breathe as she walked up to the terrace where flags waved accompaniment to triumphant music blaring from loud speakers.

As Piero Puzzi stepped on to a hastily improvised platform the music died and the crowd was silent as he began to speak.

Abbie, at the back of the crowd, was blinded by spotlights, she could just make out the dark figures around Piero. She shaded her eyes and saw him instantly. Her heart thudded — Roberto stood next to his uncle, one arm around his mother, Maria Puzzi. He was scanning the crowd intently as his uncle began to speak.

'Our Roberto has returned safe and well — trust him to pick our party night.' His voice, choked with emotion as he pushed his nephew forward to a burst of cheering.

'Thank you,' Roberto waited for the noise to die down. 'I didn't intend such a public return but once in Sicily after a secret de-briefing in Rome my first step had to be home to my family who I can't thank enough for negotiating my and my fellow hostages' release. Without Uncle Piero and his associates exerting constant pressure on the African leaders I believe the outcome of our expedition would have been very different. Thank you, Uncle Piero.'

The two men hugged and drew Maria into their embrace, and now the black-suited bodyguards set off more fireworks while waiters circulated with champagne to celebrate Roberto's return. Piero raised his glass to his nephew but Roberto was scanning the crowd again. He spoke to his mother who nodded and pointed towards Abbie.

He leapt down from the platform and struggled through the crowd with difficulty; everybody wanted to shake his hand and wish him well. He was closer to Abbie before she realised he was coming to her. She tried to turn away but he reached out for her, the crowd cleared a pathway and Abbie was in his arms.

'Thank God, you're here, I thought you might have gone back to England.' He kissed her and Abbie knew what she'd always known — she was in love with Roberto Puzzi. She kissed him back and the crowed yelled and stamped their approval.

'I thought you were engaged in the States,' Abbie murmured.

'No! That was my mother's plan to connect to the American side of her family. I can understand now why you never answered my messages.'

'Then I thought you were dead,'

Abbie hugged him closer.

He kissed her again and the crowd, still with broad smiles on their faces, melted tactfully away. 'I wasn't about to die — I had to live to ask you to marry me.'

'Oh no! I'm so sorry, I can't, I . . . '

'Why, Abbie. You love me?'

'Yes. Well, I couldn't be sure, I thought, another mistake, and now I promised . . . '

A movement behind them and a figure emerged from the shadows. 'My dear Abbie, Roberto, forgive me, a stroll, escape from the heat, and now . . . well, I couldn't help overhearing. My sincere congratulations.' Aldo's voice was warm.

'Aldo . . . '

'Ssh . . . ' he kissed her on both cheeks, 'the second I saw you together . . . you promised nothing . . . a fleeting dream . . . '

'Oh, Aldo, you've been so good to me.'

'And the business? The offer still stands, but maybe later. We shall always be friends, my girls will make sure of that. You're a lucky man, Roberto. Now I must go and join your family, I believe the partygoers are beginning to leave at last.'

'We'll follow you in a minute, Aldo.'

When Aldo had gone Roberto took Abbie's hands, the night-scented garden was now quiet. 'Just say yes, Abbie Richards, please.'

'Yes, yes, yes. I'll gladly marry you, Roberto.'

'As soon as possible, next week, tomorrow? All that time wasted in Africa, the thought of us together kept me sane.'

'But my contract, your mother?'

He laughed. 'I think we may be able to get round that, we'll rejoin the family, announce our engagement right now — and marry next week.' He kissed her tenderly and Abbie's heart swelled with love and happiness.

'Next week will be fine by me,' she said and kissed him passionately to prove it.

Of course they weren't allowed to

marry next week. Pressure from all sides ended in a compromise — a Christmas wedding to be held at Piero's villa.

Piero Puzzi, never had quite the same authority since Abbie's outburst at his lodge; the younger Puzzis had seen his authority challenged, and that challenge had shifted the power balance. Younger Puzzis felt free to question their elders, free to follow their own paths, and they loved Abbie for pushing against outdated traditions.

Piero's discomfiture was only ameliorated by Maria's decision to sell the school and land within the family.

For some reason unknown to Abbie, Piero credited her with Maria's decision and was for ever grateful.

Maria's version of events was different. 'I'm too tired to struggle against Piero's heavy mob . . . the police raid . . . the fire . . . Guiseppe who more or less admitted that Piero had paid him to start 'a small incendiary'. But all that is nothing compared with my only son's safe return. I owe Piero a huge debt for his efforts to bring about Roberto's return so if he wants my school he can have it. I shall retire to my lovely villa in the country, grow fruit and vegetables, sit in the sun — and wait.'

'Wait? Won't you be bored?' Abbie was disappointed — Piero had won so easily.

'No. I'll be happy for a while just waiting . . . waiting for my next job!'

'Job? But . . . ' Both Roberto and Abbie looked puzzled.

'Why, the grandchildren of course — the finest job in the world. You don't know, Roberto, how I've longed to see you married and have my grandchildren.

She looked fondly at Abbie. 'Didn't you tell me the other day you've always wanted a large family? Well, I've lost count of all the Puzzis, you'll be smothered at first, but you can always escape to . . . where is it, Bolden-by-the Sea? I wish you both a long and happy life, and now I'm going to pull out of hiding a bottle of the finest vintage of champagne — so don't go away.'

Once on their own Roberto took Abbie in his arms and kissed her. 'I hope you never regret joining the Puzzi clan. We could leave here if you want, settle in Australia, America, anywhere — just the two of us?'

'Goodness, no — I love you Roberto and I'll go anywhere with you but, a big family? I'd like to give that a try and, hey . . . who would we get to baby-sit in Australia?'

THE END

SUSPICIOUS HEART
EDEN IN PARADISE
SWEET CHALLENGE
FOREVER IN MY HEART
TWISTED TAPESTRIES
ALL TO LOSE
CUCKOO IN THE NEST
ROMANTIC LEGACY
LOVE'S QUEST

We do hope that you have enjoyed reading this large print book.

Did you know that all of our titles are available for purchase?

We publish a wide range of high quality large print books including:
Romances, Mysteries, Classics
General Fiction
Non Fiction and Westerns

Special interest titles available in large print are:
The Little Oxford Dictionary
Music Book, Song Book
Hymn Book, Service Book

Also available from us courtesy of Oxford University Press:
Young Readers' Dictionary
(large print edition)
Young Readers' Thesaurus
(large print edition)

For further information or a free brochure, please contact us at:
Ulverscroft Large Print Books Ltd.,
The Green, Bradgate Road, Anstey,
Leicester, LE7 7FU, England.
Tel: (00 44) **0116 236 4325**
Fax: (00 44) **0116 234 0205**

Other titles in the
Linford Romance Library:

THE HOUSE ON THE SHORE

Toni Anders

Roderick Landry, a war artist suffering the after-effects of the trenches, stays for a few weeks at the Cornish hotel where Elvina Simmons lives with her aunts Susie and Tilly. Initially reserved, Roderick eventually warms to Elvina and to life in the sleepy little seaside village. And when, together, they renovate the ruined house on the shore, it seems that their friendship may deepen — to love.

MO85

JUST IN TIME
FOR CHRISTMAS

Moyra Tarling

Vienna was just a girl when she came to live with Tobias Sheridan and his son, Drew. But when a bitter family feud sent Drew packing, he'd left town, unaware of Vienna's secret passion for him . . . Now he was back. A widower, Drew had returned for the holidays with the grandson his father had never known. But when he took the lovely, grown-up Vienna in his arms, he knew he'd come home at last — just in time for Christmas.